The Cats that Stopped the Magic

Abra's Story

Karen Anne Golden

Copyright

This book or eBook is a work of fiction.

New York's Catskills region and Oyster Bay, New York, are real places, but the characters I created do not exist, nor have they ever lived there.

Names, characters, places and incidents are products of my imagination or are used fictitiously. Any resemblance to actual events, locales, persons or cats, living or dead, is entirely coincidental.

Edited by Vicki Braun

Book cover concept by Karen Anne Golden

Graphic design by Rob W.

Table of Contents

Introduction

LATE FEBRUARY 2013

Before Katherine Moved to Erie, Indiana

From *The Cats that Surfed the Web*

Katherine Kendall's attorney turned off the Indianapolis airport road onto the ramp to the interstate. The Honda roared into traffic. "I'd like to hear the rest of your story about the magician's cat," Mark asked curiously. "How old was he when you got him?"

"Her. Scout's a girl," she corrected.

"Sorry," he said.

Katherine smiled. "Scout worked for two years for Harry's Hocus-Pocus Magic Show and was professionally known as Cadabra. Her sister was named Abra. When Scout, I mean Cadabra, was two, Harry was performing in a luxury resort in the Catskills. And while the Siamese were backstage in their traveling carrier, someone stole Abra. Harry called the police, who tried their best to find her, but their search was in vain. Abra had simply vanished. Harry and Scout never saw the other Siamese again."

"That's too bad," Mark commented.

"Scout was so traumatized by the loss of her littermate, she began slipping up in her performances, so Harry retired her."

"So that's when you came into the picture?" Mark asked.

"Not exactly. Harry gave her to a co-worker of mine, Monica DeSutter, who is currently my boss. Monica didn't have a clue about how to take care of a cat, let alone a Siamese with a behavior problem. She was constantly calling me and asking my advice on what to do. I must admit Cadabra was a handful, and even I didn't have the answers to many of her questions."

"Did Monica throw in the towel and give her to you?"

"Cadabra was with Monica for less than a year when she called me, in the middle of the night, and begged me to take her. I could hear Cadabra shrieking in the background. She sounded like a wild animal. I said I wasn't sure. I'd have to think about it."

"I'm surprised," he said. "I'd think that you'd jump at the opportunity to have a Siamese, considering the fact you have several now."

"I explained to Monica that I had just moved into my apartment and I was afraid Cadabra's shrieks would disturb my new neighbors."

"So how did Monica persuade you to take the Siamese?"

"The next morning, the doorman to my apartment building buzzed my intercom and said I'd better get downstairs ASAP . . ."

Katherine quickly sketched her first meeting with Scout for the inquisitive attorney. With her voice telling the tale on autopilot, Katherine's mind replayed all the details of that day in October 2009.

"B-z-z-z-z." The intercom blared from the end of the hall. Katherine rushed to answer. She punched the button, "Yes?"

The doorman's voice answered, "Ms. Kendall, it's Mario. You'd better come downstairs right away. This lady dropped off a present for you, and it's screaming."

She pressed the talk button, "A screaming present? That's a first. Coming right down."

Katherine waited impatiently for the elevator, and when it hadn't come in what seemed like an eternity, she rushed to the stairwell and bolted down twenty-two flights of stairs. She flew out the service door leading to the marble-floored lobby, luxuriously decorated with colonial furnishings. Mario, the Italian doorman with jet-black hair and blue eyes, wore a concerned expression on his face.

"What is it?" Katherine asked, out of breath.

"I think it's a cat," he said.

Mario had placed the cat carrier on top of his reception desk at the front entrance.

Katherine peered inside. "It's a Siamese. Did a woman named Monica DeSutter bring this?" she demanded, hand-on-hip.

"Hiss," the cat inside the carrier snarled.

"I'm sorry. I didn't get her name," Mario apologized. "She did say the cat's name was Cada —"

"Cadabra," Katherine finished.

The Siamese began rocking the cat carrier back and forth and wailing in shrill, mournful cries.

"I don't think it likes that name," Mario suggested.

"She," Katherine corrected. "Cadabra is a girl cat."

The Siamese emitted a throaty growl.

"Ms. Kendall," Mark said, interrupting the remembrance.

"Oh, I'm sorry," Katherine said, waking from her reverie. "What were you saying?"

"When did you decide to name her 'Scout?'"

"It was a few days after I got her. At night she patrols my apartment like she's on a reconnaissance mission. She's prowled so much, she's developed calluses on her paws."

"What kind of magic tricks does Scout do?"

"When you say Abracadabra, she arches her back and dances like a Halloween cat."

"You're kidding," Mark said.

"I don't say it very often because it seems to upset her."

"Maybe it brings back a sad memory."

Chapter One

Katherine "Katz" Cokenberger, a thirty-year-old heiress to millions, leaned against the kitchen counter in her guest house. She sipped hazelnut coffee and gazed affectionately at her seven felines; all had assumed their favorite spots in front of the large kitchen window.

Scout and Abra, two Siamese, seal-point sisters with an extraordinary ability to predict the future, stood tall on the extra-wide windowsill. Lilac, a vivacious lilac-point Siamese and her best buddy, Abby, a ruddy-ticked Abyssinian, sprawled out on the overhead window valance. Seal-points Iris, Dewey and Crowie snuggled in their large cozy bed near the hot-water radiator by the window.

Four months had gone by since Katherine, her husband, Jake, and their cats lived in the pink Queen Anne mansion, built in 1897. Margie Cokenberger, master old-house restorer, hadn't foreseen multiple setbacks in the attic renovation, which complicated Jake's and Katherine's plans to move back. The couple didn't relish living in a

7

house under construction with seven cats that would be disturbed by the comings and goings of workers, so they rented a farmhouse in the country. But after staying in the farmhouse for only a few months, they had to move. The rural property, with the dumbwaiter the Siamese were so fond of, had sold. Katherine and Jake had thirty days to move out, and did so on one of the coldest Indiana days of the season, with six inches of fresh snow covering a glaze of ice on country roads.

The 1912 guest house, a restored, red-brick Craftsman, was the perfect place to move into, since it was already furnished. The cats loved the all-season sun porch, which had become their new playroom.

Jake walked into the kitchen and slid onto one of the benches under the corner table. "Good morning, Sweet Pea," he greeted. "Hi, kids," he said to the cats.

The cats ignored him, except for Dewey, who looked up and belted a loud, "Mao."

"Good morning to you, too," Jake winked.

Katherine walked over to the trio in the cozy bed and asked, "Which one of you punks moved the cozy closer to the radiator?" She tugged the bed further away from it.

Iris woke up and yowled guiltily.

"I know it was you, Fredo," Katherine teased. "Listen, you can't keep moving the bed against it. You'll be toasted."

"Yowl," Iris sassed.

Scout and Abra stood up on their hind legs and dangled their front paws, doing their meerkat pose on the windowsill. They began chattering at something in the yard.

Katherine looked out the window to see what the fuss was about. The object of the Siamese's rapt attention was a squirrel, hanging upside-down on the bird feeder.

"At-at-at-at," Scout chattered.

Katherine snickered. "Jake, dear, I thought you bought a squirrel-proof feeder."

"There's no such thing," he laughed. "Have you had breakfast?"

"No, I was waiting on you. Did I ever tell you that you make the best blueberry pancakes?"

"Shucks, no, pumpkin, I ain't never heard ya say that before," he kidded in an exaggerated country accent. "I've got time to rustle up a few."

"Great, rustle up a couple for me," she answered, laughing.

Jake got up and headed to the refrigerator. Opening the door, he rummaged around for the blueberries. Not finding them, he said, "We've got a problem here."

"What?"

"We ain't got no blueberries."

Katherine laughed. "Stop it already. Your fake accent is killing me."

Jake changed the subject, and returned to his normal tone of voice. "Not that I've been snooping around your office or anything, but why are you researching insurance fraud?"

"Insurance fraud? I'm not," she said, with a bewildered expression on her face.

"I had to fetch my phone from your office—"

"What was it doing in my office?"

"One of our cats keeps taking it off the charger, and moving it to your office."

"I can only think of one cat that would do that."

"She's one of the brown-masked thieves on the windowsill, right?" Jake chuckled, then said, "Anyway there's an insurance fraud article in the *Times* today. I didn't read it. I just saw the title."

"*The New York Times*?"

Jake nodded. "It's up right now on your computer screen, in case you want to read it."

Katherine looked confused. "My computer screen? I haven't been near my computer since last night."

"Well, maybe one of the cats did their surf-the-web thing."

Abra sprung off the windowsill and ran over to Katherine. She stretched up her slender brown paws to be held.

Katherine picked her up and kissed her on the neck. "Is there something online you want your mommy to see?"

Abra struggled to be free.

"Okay, okay. Stop kicking me," Katherine said, setting Abra down. The Siamese ran out of the room.

Katherine followed her. "Where are you going?"

Abra darted into the bedroom that Katherine used as an office. She leaped on the desk, carefully stepped around the keyboard, and tapped the mouse. The computer screen refreshed itself.

"Oh, no, you didn't just do that," Katherine said, amused.

"Raw," Abra cried impatiently.

"My goodness, little girl, give me a second," Katherine said, sitting down on her office chair.

Jake came in and stood behind her. "Anything of interest?"

She began to read out loud, "Harry DeSutter—"

Jake interrupted. "Wait, isn't he the magician we went to see in Chicago?"

"The one and only," Katherine said, swiveling her chair to face Jake. "Do you remember when Abra, right in the middle of her performance, jumped off the stage and fetched a cell phone in the audience?" she asked with a twinkle in her eye.

"Jumping? I'd call it more like soaring. She had her paws stretched out like Superman," Jake laughed.

"That was the funny part, but it wasn't a joke when we went backstage and Harry was screaming at her," Katherine countered.

"Agreed. What about him?"

Katherine turned back and faced her screen. "He's being investigated for insurance fraud."

"What kind of claim would a magician file with an insurance company?"

Abra moved in front of the computer screen, reared up on her hind legs, and touched the screen.

"Abra, really? I can't see, sweetie. Jake, can you hold her?"

Jake scooped Abra from the desk and cradled her in his arms. "Do you remember this man, baby girl?"

Abra nestled her face in the fold of his arm. "Katz, read it to me. I'm busy."

"Busy, like holding Abra?"

"Something like that."

"In 2009, Harry DeSutter, stage name Magic Harry, insured one of his performers for a large sum of money. When the cat went missing . . . oh my word, Jake, I wonder if the cat was Abra."

"By the way she's acting, I'd say 'Yes.' Read the rest."

"During a performance in the Catskills, the cat was stolen from its carrier backstage."

Scout trotted into the room and jumped on the desk. She nuzzled Katherine's hand. "Ma-waugh," she cried in the affirmative. Katherine petted her, then continued, "A thorough police investigation didn't turn up any leads."

"Where was Harry when the cat disappeared?"

"Ah, just a second," she said, scanning the next paragraph. "It says that Mr. DeSutter was finished with his show and was taking a final bow in front of the audience. When he went backstage, he discovered the cat carrier only had one cat in it, when there should have been two. When he reported the theft, he accused his cat handler of stealing the feline."

"Well, did he do it?"

"No, *she* didn't. When the police questioned her, she had a firm alibi. In fact, everyone connected to the show had solid alibis."

"Why didn't the thief steal both cats? Why not just pick up the cat carrier and walk off with it?" Jake asked skeptically.

"I don't know. Harry offered a reward for the safe return of the cat. After a few months, he filed an insurance claim and collected one-hundred-thousand dollars."

"Gone, cat, gone," Jake noted. "Magic Harry collects big bucks. Isn't that rather a lot for a cat?"

"I guess Harry regarded the cat as an integral part of his show."

"Go on," Jake said, interested. "Keep reading."

"Several days before the theft, Mr. DeSutter increased the amount of coverage on the cat."

"Wow, that's suspicious."

"Four years later, the cat turned up at a Long Island animal shelter."

"That's quite a way from the Catskills."

"Oh, here we go," Katherine said excitedly. "I'm quoting here. "The *Siamese cat*," she emphasized, "had been microchipped, which allowed the shelter to locate the cat's owner, who was—"

"Drum roll, please. Let me guess . . . Harry DeSutter. And, the stolen cat was Abra," Jake said.

"Ma-waugh," Scout cried, jumping down.

"The cat was a Siamese, but the article doesn't state the cat's name," Katherine paused, then said, "It must have been Abra. We know she was stolen from a carrier she shared with Scout, I mean, at that time, Cadabra. Do you think Harry orchestrated the theft?"

"When we met him, Harry came across as an overbearing jerk, not a thief."

"Once the cat was back with the magician, Harry failed to advise the insurance company about the return."

"If he'd reported it, he'd probably have to pay back the money. I don't know how these things work."

"Maybe he spent it all, and didn't have the money to pay them back," Katherine suggested.

"I wonder what raised the red flag with the insurance company," Jake asked.

"It's a mystery. Harry is a celebrity. He didn't hide the fact that Abra was back. Remember the poster outside the theater in Chicago? It said something like Abra, the amazing Siamese, returns after her disappearance."

"After her mysterious disappearance," Jake added.

"Maybe someone in the audience was from the insurance company and put two-and-two together."

Scout hissed.

"It's okay, magic cat. You'll never see the magician again."

Jake kneaded Abra's neck, then asked, "How long did you say Abra was missing from Magic Harry?"

"Four years. I wonder where she was that entire time. Abra, if only you could talk. We'd love to know. Maybe you can surf up a clue," Katherine joked.

"Raw," Abra cried weakly. She went limp in Jake's arms.

"Katz, there's something wrong with her," Jake said, rushing to the bed. He carefully laid the Siamese down.

"What?" Katherine sprang out of her chair. "What's going on?"

"She's had some kind of collapse."

Scout hopped on the bed, and nudged Abra on the neck. Abra didn't move. Then Scout leaped to the floor, arched her back, and began swaying back-and-forth in the death dance.

Katherine sat down next to Abra. She ran her hand over the Siamese. "Jake, what's wrong with her? She's not moving."

"Maybe she's having some kind of seizure."

"We've got to get her to the vet," Katherine choked, with tears forming in her eyes.

"I'll get the carrier."

"There isn't any time. Go start the Jeep. I'll be right behind you."

Jake darted out of the room.

Katherine yanked a cozy baby blanket off the bed, then carefully wrapped Abra in it.

Abra came to, and moaned.

"Are you okay?" Katherine asked, petting her.

Abra crossed her blue eyes and smacked her lips like she'd tasted something unpleasant.

"Na-waugh," Scout cried sadly.

Chapter Two

EARLY MAY 2009

Olivia Lincoln, a sixty-four-year-old resident of
Oyster Bay, Long Island, sat on a Mission-style chair, and
looked out her first-floor bedroom window at the gardener.
He should have been weeding her iris bed, but instead was
chatting up the young, attractive nurse who had been sent
by the in-home nursing agency. Olivia slid the window
open and yelled, "Hey, I don't pay you people to dillydally
around."

The couple outside was so engaged in their
conversation, they didn't hear her, and continued talking.

In 2007, Olivia had been diagnosed with a rare form
of thyroid cancer, which had been treated with radiation
and chemotherapy. She'd been cancer-free for two years,
but just recently the cancer had reappeared. Roland, her
husband of thirty years, was devastated by the news, and
spent most of his time surfing the Internet for miracle
cures.

The couple lived in a three-story, Beaux-Arts mansion built in the roaring twenties by Olivia's grandfather, Preston, who made his fortune in the stock market. When the market crashed, he made even more money by buying up real estate from his fellow bankers, who'd decided selling was a better way to limit their financial losses than jumping out of tall buildings.

Tragically, in the 1930s, Preston was hit by a car speeding down Broadway in front of Macy's department store. He died in a hospital several days later. His wife, Bradley, Olivia's grandmother, raised four children, three girls and one boy. Humphrey, Olivia's father, inherited the house and married a woman of independent wealth. The couple had one daughter, Olivia.

Although Olivia was born into money, she didn't let the inheritance interfere with her ambition. She chose a career in banking. She graduated from Harvard University with an advanced degree in finance. For a number of years, she worked on Wall Street as a financial whiz — an uncommon vocation for a young woman in the early 1980s.

She not only increased her personal fortune, but also benefitted a long list of investment bankers she'd worked for. Life had been good to her. She was happy in her job, and happy in her marriage. That was until the cancer appeared.

Getting even more annoyed with the gardener flirting with the nurse, Olivia screamed out the window. "Jack, shut up and let the nurse come inside."

Jack, the gardener, apologized, "I'm sorry, Mrs. Lincoln."

Olivia threw him a dirty look and closed the window.

The twenty-something nurse rushed in the house, and was shown to Olivia's bedroom by one of the house maids.

"I'm so sorry," the nurse said, bustling in.

Olivia commented, "You look awfully young to be a registered nurse."

The nurse was taken aback by the comment, then answered, "I just graduated from school."

"I need my pain pill," Olivia ordered. "I need it *now*," she said, with a strong emphasis on the last word.

The young woman scanned the room for the logical place medicine would be stored. Not finding it, she said timidly, "Where are they?"

"Over there, by the door, on the marble-top chest."

The nurse walked to the chest and fumbled for the right bottle. Earlier, the agency had given her a list of Olivia's medicines, but she hadn't had time to familiarize herself with the dosage and time schedule.

Roland walked in and noticed his wife's distressed look and the nurse's troubled expression. "Hello, I'm Roland, Olivia's husband," he introduced. "Are you the new nurse from the agency?"

The woman nodded, with eyes-wide-open in expectation that she would be fired any second.

"I need my pain med and this incompetent girl—"

Roland put his hand up, "Stop! Olivia, we've talked about this." He turned to the nurse. "Could you wait for me outside in the atrium?"

"What's an atrium?" she asked, stuttering.

"Just outside the door. Make yourself comfortable. I'll only be a minute."

The woman nodded and hurried out of the room.

Roland found the right combination of drugs and placed the pills in his wife's hand. He poured a glass of water and handed it to her.

Olivia swallowed the pills, then sheepishly looked up at her husband. "She should've been in here earlier, but she chose to flirt with that man you hired for the gardening."

"We've had this conversation before. The agency said if this nurse didn't work out, there was a strong possibility we'd have to go to another agency. Do you really want to do that?"

"I don't want to be difficult," Olivia explained. "I'm just frustrated that I'm stuck in this room not able to do the things I've always loved to do. You know I never let anyone get near my iris bed. I always did the flower gardens."

"I know, darling," he said gently, sitting down in the chair beside her. He took her hand. "Maybe you need a companion."

"I don't need a companion," she said indignantly. "I have you."

"That's not what I meant. I mean since Duchess died, you've been depressed, and quite frankly, so irritable sometimes you're really hard to be around."

"That bad?" she asked sadly.

Roland nodded.

"Duchess was the sweetest Siamese in the world," Olivia choked, and brought her hand up to wipe a tear from her eye. "I miss her so much."

Roland kissed her hand. "Now, now, dearest, don't cry. I miss her, too."

"I'm still in shock. She was only two. I can't believe that our precious Siamese died of cancer. Roland, am I a cancer magnet?"

Roland shook his head, then said, "Why don't I find you another Siamese? How about a sweet little kitten? Would that make you happy, dear?"

"I'm not sure a kitten would be a good idea. I'm not long for this world. When I'm gone to the grave, do you really want to be raising a young cat?" she asked gloomily.

Roland gave a pained, dejected look. "Long for the world," he repeated sadly. "You don't know that. The doctors said you need to undergo chemo again."

"What? Lose my hair a second time? Forget that," she answered, then laughed. "I just got my hair to look halfway-decent."

Roland leaned over and kissed his wife on the cheek. "I think your hair looks wonderful, and your sense of humor will get you through this."

"I know it will."

"Okay then, I better go out and smooth things over with the new nurse. Be back in a minute."

Olivia gave another sheepish look. "She left several minutes ago."

"What?" Roland said, getting up and looking out the window.

"She's gone. She must have had the car service wait for her. She's probably calling the agency right now and telling them what a monster I am," Olivia continued.

"I better call them," Roland said, extracting his cell phone from his belt holder. "What was the gal's name?"

"I didn't get to that part."

Roland punched in the agency's number. He started to leave the room.

"Wait," Olivia called. "Tell the agency I want a more mature nurse. Not a young whippersnapper just out of nursing school."

"I can't do that."

"Why?"

"That's age discrimination."

"You're a master of words. Figure something out."

"Why does age matter?" Roland asked.

"I just feel I have nothing in common with twenty-somethings. The last nurse I interviewed didn't even know who Alfred Hitchcock was."

Roland laughed. "Actually, the age of the nurse doesn't have anything to do with it. You just want a movie buff like you."

"Yes, that's it, exactly," Olivia agreed. "Oh, and Roe, I love your idea about the Siamese, but not a kitten. I want a cat that looks like Duchess."

"Duchess might be a hard act to follow, but I'll certainly give it a try," Roland smiled, then started speaking into the phone. He stepped outside and quietly shut the door.

Chapter Three

LATE MAY 2009

New York's Catskills, Four-Star Resort Hotel

Magic Harry's Hocus-Pocus Show

Friday before Rehearsal

Stagehand Emma Thomas, also known as "the cat wrangler," walked onto the stage, carrying a large cat carrier. Inside two svelte Siamese cats, littermates, stood tall, looking through the front metal gate. Emma gently set the carrier down and said to the cats, "We're here." She pulled a hair-scrunchie from her purse and tied her long, blond hair into a ponytail. "Hello, Roy," she called to the middle-aged man who was standing nearby.

Roy, the animal trainer with shoulder-length, brown hair and piercing gray eyes, stood behind a specially designed magician's box, which had a hinged metal arm at the back, attached to an electric circular saw. "How's it going?" he asked, walking to the front of the box and rearranging two barstools.

"I'll be able to tell you as soon as I get my hearing back," she complained.

"What's wrong with your hearing?"

"It took me several hours to drive from Nyack, and the Siamese shrieked the entire time."

"I warned ya. Siamese are one of the more vocal breeds. But, what are you complaining about? At least you have a car. It takes me two trains and a bus to get to where I'm going on Long Island."

"I didn't sleep very well last night, either," Emma continued, yawning.

"Why's that?"

"My grandmother lives in this huge Victorian house on the Hudson. She insisted the Siamese be shut up in a room because she didn't want her precious antiques destroyed."

"I bet that didn't go over well with the cats."

"They howled like banshees until my Grammy couldn't stand it anymore. She let them out, and then the cat version of the steeplechase race began. I swear the Siamese ran for hours."

"Good exercise for them," Roy smiled.

"This went on for hours."

Roy snickered, then said coyly, "You volunteered to take them home with you. The hotel has excellent accommodations for our animals."

"Are you kidding? A three-by-three cage is not my idea of 'excellent accommodations.' I didn't want them cooped up in a cage. They're only two-years-old and still as active as kittens. I love them to death, but—"

Roy interrupted, "How did you get them to quiet down?"

"I put them in my bedroom and they slept with me."

"Wish I'd been there," Roy said in a flirty manner.

"Stop it!" Emma said, throwing Roy a dirty look. "I'm not a fan of your innuendos."

"Just kidding," Roy said, walking over to the carrier. He looked inside. "How are my little girlfriends?" he spoke to the cats in a soft voice.

"Waugh," the one cat cried. "Raw," the other one chimed in.

Roy took on a serious tone. "Emma, I need to remind you of something."

"What?"

"In our line of business, we don't get attached to the animals. There will come a day when Harry retires the Siamese and moves on to other cats. Are you going to be able to psychologically handle that?"

"What, are you a shrink?" Emma asked, rolling her eyes. "I'm not attached to them. It's just that this gig is driving distance from my Grammy's, and the cats can take a break from being on the road."

"Okay, don't say I didn't warn you."

"Back to business, do you have everything you need? I brought spare clickers. Oh, and I made those tuna cat treats the Siamese love. Anything else you want me to bring before the performance this weekend?"

"No, Ms. Emma," he said, looking her up-and-down in a suggestive manner.

"Cut it out," she said irritably. "What would your new wife think about you flirting with me?"

Roy stepped back, "Aren't you in a mood?"

"I'm sick of you coming on to me. I don't date married men."

"Who said I'd want to date you," he squinted, lying. "Besides, it's not a secret that you're sweet on Harry."

"Enough," she said indignantly. "Let me start this conversation over," Emma pronounced, annoyed. "I haven't had a chance to talk to Harry this morning; are the Siamese learning anything new today?"

"I'll be teaching the Siamese a scaredy-cat routine."

"Why do you want the Siamese to act scared?"

"Not petrified scared, but a dramatic startle. Harry wants the cats to sway back-and-forth and screech loudly. Then arch their backs and dance around. I've got to make this happen lickety-split."

"Sounds fun," Emma said, with a look of wonder. "What part of the show will they be doing this in?"

"Before Harry saws the woman in two," Roy chuckled.

"Ew, Roy. That's gross."

"Well, that's the illusion."

"What are the cats supposed to do?"

"The Siamese will jump down from their barstools, begin their loud shrieking routine, arch their backs, and hop up-and-down like deranged Halloween cats."

"I take it there will be special eerie music for this."

"Yes, that's one of their cues."

"Why does Harry want the cats to do this?"

"To help build suspense. We want the audience to be on the edge of their seats wondering if the new girl will be cut in half."

"Wait! Did you just say new girl?"

"Some showgirl from Las Vegas. Melanie left for another gig."

"That's news to me."

"The beauty of this trick is that it will be fast and furious."

"Why will it be fast?"

"So, the audience doesn't figure out that the show gal in the box has tucked her legs out of harm's way."

"Can you walk me through my *part* in this? No pun intended."

"I sent you an email."

"I know. I'm sorry. I printed it, but didn't have a chance to read it. Remember, I had two very needy Siamese, who demanded my attention." Emma reached into her bag and pulled out a sheet of paper. Scanning the email, she said, "I'll be off-stage, left wing with the cat carrier. The showgirl . . . geez, Roy, what's the woman's name?"

"Her stage name is Bardot. Harry will introduce Bardot, who will cross the stage. She's drop-dead gorgeous, so the audience will go nuts."

"I kind of get that by the sound of her name," Emma said, tongue-in-cheek. "Then what?"

"Harry will briefly explain the act, then assist Bardot into the box. Once she's inside, he'll move to the front and open a door to show the audience that Bardot is lying flat in the box."

"Where will the cats be during this?"

"They'll be off stage in their carrier. Harry will move behind the box and start the saw, and then he'll stop and say, 'But, wait, I can't do this without my assistants: Abra and Cadabra!' That's when you release the cats from their carrier."

The Siamese began to rock the carrier.

"Stop," Roy demanded.

The Siamese yowled.

"Where's my clicker when I need it," Roy complained. "Emma hand me those treats."

Emma reached in her bag and removed a small plastic container. When she removed the lid, the Siamese began yowling louder.

Roy clicked his clicker. "Quiet," he said to the excited felines. When they settled down, he fed each one of them a treat. Then he said to Emma, "Yeah, you're right. The cats love them."

Emma smiled, then continued, "Okay, I'll be off-stage, left wing. You'll be with me, right?"

"There's been a little change. I'll be in the right wing."

"This is different. Why the change? Normally, we are together."

"I'll be on the other side, in case the cats screw up and run to the right. I'm banking that won't happen, but we don't want them running amok backstage, with the other animals."

"What other animals?"

"I meant the pigeons."

"Even if they did get back there, the pigeons are in cages. This pair would never harm the pigeons."

"Seriously? Have you forgotten the show in New Orleans? Abra ran off the stage and went directly to the birds. When I chased her down, one of the pigeons was missing and Abra had a feather sticking out of her mouth."

"Impossible. These cats like their food from a can."

"Don't forget that gig in Baltimore. The Siamese ran the wrong direction and nearly ran right out of the theater."

"That idiot stagehand shouldn't have propped the door open."

"All right, back to the plan. The cats will enter the stage left wing. Let Abra out first."

"Thanks for making my job easy," Emma said sarcastically. "You know both of them will be at the gate vying to get out."

"That's your problem. I want Abra first because she's the better of the two and rarely messes up. Cadabra will take her lead. Okay, back to the plan, let Abra out. Wait three seconds, then let Cadabra out. The cats will run, hop on their stools, and face the audience."

"You know, Roy, when the audience sees our royal pair, they'll go wild with cooing and aah-ing."

"Definitely, but once the house has quieted down, Harry will start the saw and cut the gal in half. Bardot will scream bloody murder."

"Won't her screaming scare the cats?"

"Don't think so. We'll see how they react during rehearsal."

"So, when Ms. Bardot screams, what are the Siamese doing?"

"They'll jump off their stools and perform their Halloween dance. Harry will come to the front of the box and partially open it. Stage guts and blood will pour out of the box."

"Ew," Emma said again, scrunching up her face in disgust. "Are you sure the audience will want to see that?"

"Not my decision. Magic Harry makes up the rules."

"I'm sorry I interrupted. Okay, then what?"

"The cats will run off-stage and get into their carrier," Roy answered. "On stage, Harry will open the box all the way to show that Bardot is okay. Curtain will close."

"What act is this?"

"Final act of the show."

"What about the curtain call? Will the Siamese be involved in that?"

"No, not a good idea. Don't you remember? The last time we tried it, it was a disaster. Cadabra soared off the stage and was trotting down the center aisle. It took two ushers to catch her."

Emma giggled at the memory. "I agree, probably not a good idea. But," Emma beamed, then complimented, "Roy, you're the best animal trainer I've worked with. I'm sure you could teach them to stay on stage during the curtain call."

"And do what? Fetch the roses that the audience throws on stage?" His cell phone rang the *Lion Sleeps Tonight* ringtone. He looked at the front of the phone at the name and frowned. "Excuse me. I've got to take this."

"Okay," Emma said, stooping down to check on the cats.

Roy walked away, and began pacing the floor. "Today?" he shouted in the phone. "You can't be serious.

Jimmy . . . please . . . I beg of you, stop harassing me. You'll get your money on Sunday."

Roy hung up. He walked over and put his hand on Emma's shoulder. "Can you do me a huge favor and not tell anyone what you just heard?"

"Sure, no problem. Are you in some kind of trouble?"

"Sort of. I made the mistake of borrowing money from a friend of a friend, and now he wants his money back."

"You mean you didn't borrow from a bank?" she asked, arching her eyebrows with concern.

"It goes like this, Ms. Emma," Roy began with a scowl. "Harry's a cheap bastard—"

"Shhh, you don't want Harry to hear you. You never know when he's going to pop in."

"What I'm saying is I've had some big money expenses moving my wife here from Ohio and renting that uppity place."

"What uppity place? I thought you rented from your aunt?"

"I did, but she's charging me the same rent the previous tenants paid."

"How much do you owe? Can I help? I mean, I don't have much, but . . ." her voice trailed off.

"Twenty-five thousand."

Emma's mouth dropped. "I take that back. I don't have that much."

"That's what I mean."

"Have you gone to a bank?"

Roy looked up and made a face. "Duh, do I look stupid? I went to the bank first. They wouldn't loan it to me because I have a terrible credit history."

"I didn't mean to imply that you're stupid, but this person you owe money to, please tell me it's not a loan shark?"

"He's the worst kind of shark."

"What do you mean?"

"He works for the mob."

Chapter Four

Friday before Rehearsal

Harry DeSutter, a fifty-five-year-old entertainer with dyed black hair and matching goatee, sat at the bar of the hotel's cocktail lounge. He nervously looked at the clock on the wall, and then scanned the room for the umpteenth time. His insurance man, Ethan Montero, was fifteen minutes late, and in a few minutes, Harry had to meet someone else.

Ethan, a tall, dark-haired, well-dressed man, hurried into the near-empty lounge and rushed over to Harry. "Mr. DeSutter, I must apologize. I had a problem getting a cab from the train station."

Harry shrugged, "I'm happy you're here now. Have a seat."

Ethan placed his briefcase on the floor and hopped up on the barstool next to the magician.

"Did you bring the documents I'm supposed to sign?" Harry asked.

"Yes, I did. But, let's grab a table in a minute, so you can sign them."

"That works. I've got a rehearsal in a few. How's the insurance business?"

"It's doing great. I'm not at the office much. I've been traveling a lot to clients' homes."

"That's good. How have you been? Last time we spoke you said you were getting engaged."

Ethan smiled. "I'm officially engaged."

"Have you set the date?" Harry asked.

"We're getting married in August. I do hope you'll come."

"Yes, of course, I wouldn't miss it. Congratulations. This is wonderful news. Bartender," he called to the man standing nearby, "Bring me another shot and make this young man a drink."

"What will it be?" the bartender asked, coming over.

"Dry martini," Ethan said. "Shaken, not stirred."

The bartender nodded and went to the other end of the bar to mix the drink. When he was out of earshot, Harry asked, "I've never been married. How did you know you wanted to marry . . . oh, forgive me, I've forgotten her name."

"Megan Plummer. Every time I'm near her, I feel like electricity is jolting between the two of us."

Harry tipped his head back and laughed loudly. "Sounds like something I should put in my Hocus-Pocus show."

Ethan grinned. "Speaking of your show, I know you're busy, so let's get down to business. I've increased the insurance on your Siamese performers. They're currently insured for twenty-five thousand per cat, but I've upped it to one-hundred-thousand dollars."

"Per cat?"

Ethan nodded.

"That sounds about right," Harry noted.

Ethan continued, "In the event they are accidentally killed while performing, lost in transit, or stolen, you'd be covered. But, don't mind me asking — and this is between you and me — why so much on the cats, when the insurance on your other performers is far less?"

"These cats are very special. They've become very popular with my audience, and because of that, my ticket sales have gone sky-high."

The bartender set down two drinks.

"Thank you," Harry said. "Charge this to my room. I'm in Room 216."

"Yes, sir, will do," the bartender said, moving to the cash register.

Ethan took a drink out of his glass, and then glanced at his watch, "Let's get the paperwork signed. Actually, we don't need a table. We can do it here." He slid off the barstool and picked up his briefcase. He set the case on the bar and opened it. Extracting two documents, he passed them to Harry. "Just sign here, here and here, and we're good to go."

"Does the policy change take effect immediately?"

"Since you already have other policies with us, the answer is yes. The increase in the premium will show up on your next statement. I'll get this back to the office pronto."

"I appreciate it," Harry said, then noticed the short, balding man who had just walked in. "Warren, over here."

The man approached Harry and said, "Hello. I'm a little bit early, but I thought you'd be anxious to see the new prototype drawing." He held the rolled-up drawing in his hand.

"No problem. Hey, you want to join us for a drink, then talk business?"

Ethan bowed out. "Listen, I better go." He hurriedly finished his drink.

"Before you rush off, Ethan, this is Warren. He's in charge of my props and gizmos that I use in the show."

"Hello," Ethan said, shaking Warren's hand.

"Please to meet you."

"Sorry to dash off," Ethan said, grabbing his briefcase. "It's been great to see you, Harry. Nice to meet you, Warren. Take care now," he said, leaving the lounge.

Harry called after him, "Don't do anything I wouldn't do."

Ethan was already out the door and didn't hear him.

Warren suggested to Harry, "Can we get a table? I've got the prototype drawn up. I can't wait to show you."

"Sure, of course." Harry slid off the barstool and walked to a table in the back of the lounge.

Warren unrolled the drawing and placed the nearby salt and pepper shakers on the edges to keep it flat. He began to explain, "Per your instructions, I've designed a version of your magician's box, but smaller in scale."

"What about the retractable saw blade? I want you to make sure it doesn't come anywhere near my performer."

"Oh, be assured, I'm working on that. One thing that I know for sure is the saw is much quieter than the bigger-sized one."

"Great. There are two things you must keep in mind. Number one, we don't want the saw's noise to freak out the animal. Second, we don't want to cut the animal in two."

"I assure you, everything in the design is quite safe. By the way, which animal will be in the box? I'll need measurements of their body size."

"The performer will be one of my Siamese cats. Come to the rehearsal in a few minutes and you can measure her then. Just don't tell anyone why you're doing this. Just say it's for a new costume."

"Why?"

Harry became irritated, "Because I haven't told my trainer yet about the new act."

"My lips are sealed."

"How soon can you have it made?"

"The guy who's building it said it would take a few days."

"Perfecto! Now, I must dash off. Thanks, Warren."

"You're quite welcome," Warren answered.

Chapter Five

Friday in Oyster Bay —The Interview

A black four-door sedan pulled up in front of the Beaux-Arts mansion and stopped. "Here we are," the driver announced to the passenger in the back seat.

"Are you sure this is the correct address?" the passenger asked, amazed by the grandeur of the three-story house.

"I've been on this run many times before. I'm positive."

Julia Jackson stepped out of the car service, grabbed her nurse-on-wheels bag, and thanked the driver. "How much do I owe you?" she asked.

The driver powered down his window. "Nothing, for this ride. It's on the house."

"What are you talking about?"

"I want to break the nurse curse." He exploded with laughter. "Nurse curse, that's a good one," he said, slapping the steering wheel.

"What curse is that?" Julia asked uneasily.

"It goes like this, ma'am. Every time I bring a nurse from the agency to this address, I get a call back pretty darn quick. Seems the lady of the house is hard to deal with, so I have to hurry back and pick 'em up. Lately, I've just been parking at the end of the lane, waiting for the call. I'm hoping this time, if I don't charge you anything, you won't be calling me, crying your eyes out."

"I'm a professional. I don't 'cry my eyes out.' This isn't my first rodeo. Maybe I'll have a different car service pick me up," she began firmly, "so I don't have to listen to some smart-aleck driver tell me my business."

"Okay, ma'am. Have it your way." He stepped on the gas and drove out of the circular drive.

"Nuts," Julia said under-her-breath. She climbed several steps to the mansion's front landing and stopped. She stood in awe, studying the architecture. "Wow," she said aloud. "I love this house." She rang the bell, and soon an older woman dressed in a two-piece navy-blue suit answered the door.

The woman asked, "Are you Ms. Jackson from the agency?"

"Yes," Julia answered. "Are you Mrs. Lincoln?"

"No, I'm Mrs. Lincoln's personal assistant. Please come in. Mrs. Lincoln is in the library. Follow me," the woman guided.

Julia followed, careful not to trip on the thick oriental hallway rug. Her eyes quickly scanned the foyer with the oil paintings on the wall, the Art Deco vases and lamps on the side tables. The entrance alone reminded her of one of the period rooms at the Metropolitan Museum of Art.

The assistant knocked on a door, then opened it. "Mrs. Lincoln, the nurse is here."

"Thank you, Margo. Please show her in."

Margo turned to the nurse. "You may go in, dear." As Julia stepped inside, Margo whispered, "Best of luck," then she closed the door.

Mrs. Lincoln was sitting on a red damask chair in front of a crackling fire in the fireplace. Above the mantel was a life-size portrait of a woman with a cat. Julia couldn't help but admire the gilded-framed oil painting of a woman standing with a Siamese cat perched on her shoulder.

Olivia asked, "Hello, are you Ms. Jackson?"

"Yes, but please call me Julia."

"I'm Mrs. Lincoln, but please call me Olivia." Olivia laughed, breaking the tension of an awkward introduction. "Have a seat," she said, pointing to a matching chair.

"Thank you." Julia sat down and pulled her nurse-on-wheels bag to her side. She asked, "Is that you in the portrait?"

"Why, yes, it is. I have to say, you're the first nurse I've interviewed that ever noticed it."

"I love Siamese cats," Julia said, beaming. "I grew up with one. Princess lived to be twenty-two-years-old."

"That's quite an old age. I'm sorry to say my Duchess didn't live that long," Olivia answered.

"I'm sorry," Julia said with a concerned expression. "Every time one of my beloved cats crosses the rainbow bridge, another piece of my heart is broken."

"I know the feeling all too well. Have you had many cats?"

"I'd say over the years I've had a dozen or more."

"I know it's considered rude to ask a woman her age, but how old are you?"

"I don't think it's rude. I'm fifty-four."

Olivia smiled. "Do you have any cats now?"

"No, not with me. I got married several months ago, and my husband doesn't want any pets. I left my black cat, Maggie, with my mom back home."

"That's sad."

"I know," Julia answered gloomily. "I miss my mom and my Maggie something awful."

"Where are you from? I hear a hint of an accent."

"I'm from Ohio."

"Ohio? How on earth did you end up in Oyster Bay?"

"My husband has an aunt who lives several miles from here. We rent her carriage house."

"What's her name? Perhaps I know her."

"Penelope Chadwick."

"I don't believe we've met. Is your husband from this area?"

"Actually, he's an army brat. He's lived all over the world."

"What does he do?"

"He's an animal trainer for a magician."

"Is that so?" Olivia asked curiously. "Does he work nearby?"

"Right now, Roy, that's my husband's name, is working in one of the resort hotels in the Catskills. That's where his boss has his magic show."

"Interesting," Olivia said casually.

The library door opened. Roland walked in carrying a tray with a Blue Willow design teapot and several matching cups. "Hello," he greeted. "I thought you two might enjoy a cup of tea."

"How sweet," Olivia said.

"Thank you," Julia said. "You're very kind."

"Roland, this is Julia," Olivia introduced. "I've decided she would be perfect for the job because we have something in common."

"What's that?" Roland grinned. He was happy the interview was going well.

"Julia loves cats, and she once had a Siamese."

"Imagine that," Roland said, setting down the tray on the small table between the two chairs. "Julia, I'm the husband."

"I apologize for my manners. This is my husband, Roland. Roland, this is Julia Jackson."

Julia smiled. "I'm pleased to meet you."

Olivia said, "Roe, Julia is the first nurse to ever notice the painting. Can you tell her the story about it?"

"I'd love to hear it." Julia leaned forward with interest.

"I'd be glad to tell it in just a minute." Roland reached down and poured tea into two cups. "My Olivia takes her tea with a lump of sugar," he said, dropping a cube of sugar into her cup. How about you, Julia?"

"I take it plain."

"Plain?" he asked.

"I mean no sugar, please."

Roland handed a cup to Olivia and then Julia. He walked over to the portrait. "I commissioned this painting from a local artist. My Olivia, when she felt better, volunteered at the mission's soup kitchen. Every time she went, she'd take Duchess along with her. Duchess loved to ride—"

"On my shoulder," Olivia finished. "Duchess made so many people happy. Everyone wanted to talk to her or pet her. My darling Siamese loved it."

"Mrs. Lincoln, that is such a wonderful story," Julia admired.

"Please, call me Olivia. Now, Julia, do you accept the position?"

Julia was surprised by the sudden offer. "Don't you want to see my résumé?"

"No, that won't be necessary. If the agency cleared you, I'm sure your credentials are just fine."

Julia smiled. "If you don't mind, I have a few questions. I was told that the hours would be nine to five, Monday through Friday. Is that correct?" she asked.

"That works for me."

"And, can you tell me my duties?"

Olivia took a sip, then said, "Basic nursing. I'd expect you to make sure I take my meds on time and make sure I eat. Sometimes I forget to eat. It would be nice to have a schedule. Oh, and go with me to doctor and treatment appointments."

"Sounds right up my alley, but I should tell you right off the bat, I don't have a car."

Roland piped in, "We have a driver who will take you wherever Olivia needs to go."

Julia's eyes grew big. "For real?" she asked, then fumbled, "I mean I've never worked for anyone who had a personal driver."

Olivia and Roland glanced at each other, and then laughed.

Roland said, "We're a little bit spoiled."

Olivia asked, "One more thing. Do you like old movies?"

Julia grinned. "Yes, I do. My husband teases me and calls me a movie buff."

Olivia laughed. "That's what Roe calls me. Who is your favorite Hollywood director of the past?" she quizzed.

Julia thought, then said, "It would have to be Alfred Hitchcock."

Olivia clapped her hands. "Mine, too. Oh, we'll get along splendidly. Please, Julia, say you'll be my new nurse."

Yes," Julia said, smiling. "When shall I begin?"

"Right now. Can you stay until five?"

"Yes, of course."

Roland moved toward the door. "I'll call the agency with the happy news."

"Wonderful," Olivia said with a grin.

Chapter Six

Back in the Catskills

Emma walked to Harry's dressing room. She was concerned about Roy being in debt to a loan shark and wanted to get Harry's take on things. She also wanted an opportunity to talk to Harry alone. Since Bardot had showed up on the scene, Harry hadn't paid any attention to her. Emma was crushed because she'd always been Harry's favorite. Now, she felt she'd been replaced by a Vegas bombshell.

She knocked on the door. "Harry? It's Emma. Can I have a word with you before rehearsal?"

Harry didn't answer.

Emma tested the doorknob, and found it wasn't locked. She gently opened the door. She scanned the small room, and when she found Harry wasn't there, she stepped inside. Her eyes were drawn to a side table with a blueprint lying on top of it. She walked over to the drawing and studied it. Hand-drawn with blue ink was a small version of the magician's box. She read the description out loud: "Cat will be placed in box. Its back legs will be braced as shown." She couldn't read any more. She couldn't believe her eyes. Her face clouded with anger.

"Oh, no," she said, horrified. "I've got to stop this."

"Stop what?" Harry asked, entering the room. "Hey, what are you doing looking at my stuff?"

"Harry, you've gone too far. You can't do this."

"Oh, really? So you're the boss now."

Emma stood her ground. "Your audience will hate this, and hate you for doing it."

"It's just a routine with the Siamese."

"Cadabra will never stand for this."

"Who said I was using Cadabra. It's Abra. Roy will train her to do it, and if she can't do the trick, I'll find another cat that will. The animal shelter is full of cats begging to be adopted."

"I'm pretty much sure if you go through with this, the animal welfare people will be on you like a tick on a deer. And if . . . if . . . Abra dies or is hurt," she stammered. "You'll go to jail!"

"Out!" Harry shouted angrily. "Get out of my dressing room, before I throw you out. If I find out you've mentioned this to anyone, I'll fire you so fast your head will spin."

Emma was taken aback by Harry's loud burst of anger. "Fine," she said, storming out, slamming the door behind her.

She refused to keep this a secret. She had to find Roy. First, she checked his dressing room. When she didn't find him there, she rushed to the small kitchen area. Warren sat at one of the tables, drinking a cup of coffee.

Emma walked over to him. She stood with her arms crossed. "How dare you design that cat version of the magician's box," she accused angrily.

"Frankly, I don't see how this is any of your business," he replied smugly.

"I'm making it my business. I'm going to make sure no cats will ever be part of this trick."

"I only do what I'm paid to do. Why don't you do the same and mind your own business. So, if that's all, why don't you take a flying leap and get out of my face."

"Jerk," Emma said, stomping off.

She nearly bumped into one of the stagehands. "Have you seen Roy?"

"Watch where you're going," he said, annoyed.

"I'm looking for Roy. Have you seen him?" she asked again, this time with an irritated tone in her voice.

"He's on-stage. Isn't that where you're supposed to be?" the stagehand asked sarcastically.

Emma glanced at her watch. "Oh, no, I'm late. Listen, thanks for the info." She ran to the stage area and found Roy.

The Siamese cats were on their barstools, standing tall, until they saw Emma. Then Cadabra leaped down and ran over to her.

Emma picked her up. "Little girl, you've got to go back to the stool."

Roy said, aggravated, "Set her down, Emma. Cadabra. Back," he said, clicking his clicker.

"Waugh," Cadabra meowed in a troubled voice.

"Now!" Roy commanded.

Cadabra raced to the stool, jumped up, and stood tall. Roy moved over and gave her a treat.

"Good girl," he praised, then to Emma, "While you were at lunch, I taught the cats the scaredy-cat routine."

"You did? You should have let me know. I wanted to be here."

"Sorry about your luck."

"Roy, I've got to talk to you before Harry shows up."

"Why?"

"Harry is having a magician's box made for a cat, and he's adamant that Abra will do the sawing-in-half trick."

"That's nuts. He can't do that."

"But, he is. I saw the drawing of the horrific thing in his dressing room."

"Snooping? Or was it a chance meeting with the boss?" Roy asked facetiously.

"I wasn't snooping," Emma defended. "I wanted to talk to him before the rehearsal. He wasn't there. I couldn't help but notice the drawing."

"It seems to me it would be dangerous for an animal to do this trick."

"I know. I can only think of the unspeakable things that could happen if Abra didn't do what she was trained to do."

"Calm down. I'll act surprised when Harry tells me about it, then I'll try to talk him out of it."

"Okay, you're the best."

Roy winked. "I'll take that as a compliment," then he added, "That explains something."

"Explains what?"

"That Warren guy was just here. He took a measurement of Abra. When I asked him why, he said it was for a new costume."

"Yeah, right," Emma spit. "I just spoke to him in the break room. He told me to mind my own business."

"Warren is always trying to get brownie points with the boss. Where's Harry now?"

"I left him in his dressing room."

"Hello, Roy," Harry greeted, walking across the stage. He had a bounce in his step. He ignored Emma.

Bardot joined them, center-stage. "Good afternoon, everyone," she said in a gravelly voice. She had a beautiful mane of long, blonde hair.

Harry made introductions. "Bardot, this is Roy, my animal trainer, and this is Emma, my royal pain-in-the-neck."

Bardot looked surprised. "Why is this young girl a pain-in-the-neck?" she asked Harry.

Harry didn't answer.

Emma's face reddened. "It's nice to meet you."

"Likewise. I've already met Roy," Bardot said.

"Enough with the introductions, let's get the show on the road," Harry said. "Roy, put the cats back in their carrier. We'll start from the beginning."

"But that's my job," Emma protested.

Roy grabbed her by the arm. "Come on."

They left the stage and stood by the carrier. Roy clicked his clicker and the Siamese jumped off their stools. They ran off-stage, side-by-side, like two horses in a Roman chariot race.

Roy opened the carrier's gate and the cats dashed inside. He quickly latched it.

Emma said to Roy in a quiet voice. "What are we going to do? If Harry goes through with this, and something terrible happens to Abra, I'll never forgive myself. I swear, if he kills her, I'll murder him."

"Calm down, Emma. Don't let anyone hear you say that."

"I'm just so upset."

"Don't worry. I'll figure something out."

"Raw," Abra commiserated.

"It's okay, sweetie," Emma consoled the Siamese, then said to Roy, "I love her so much."

"I know you do," Roy said, hugging her.

Harry yelled. "Hey, you two, what's the hold up? I don't have all day."

Roy squeezed the spring-loaded latch and opened the gate. He said to the Siamese, "One . . . two . . . three, now, go—go—go."

The cats flew back onto the stage and sprang to their barstools.

Up above the stage, in the sound booth, an engineer flipped a switch and eerie music began to play. The cats swiveled their ears forward and then backwards, in dislike of the music, which sounded like a modern twist on a 1950's Sci-Fi score.

Cadabra sneezed at Bardot's strong perfume, and assumed a meerkat stance. She stood up on her hind legs, dangled her forepaws, and sniffed the air. She turned her head to face Bardot, then she sneezed a second time.

Harry called to Roy. "Why's she doing that?"

"She must be allergic to Bardot's cheap perfume," Roy said glibly.

"Now wait a minute, Mister," Bardot protested. "My perfume ain't cheap."

"That's what you call perfume?" Harry asked, joining in on the joke. "It smells more like bug spray. Sorry, my dear, don't wear it on stage anymore. We can't have the cats sneezing during a performance."

Bardot gave a dejected look. "You're the boss."

Cadabra sneezed one last time.

*   *   *

After the rehearsal, Emma packed up the Siamese, and bungeed their cat carrier to a rolling luggage cart. Roy stepped over and said, "Maybe you should leave the cats here tonight?"

"Why? I'm taking them to my Grammy's house."

"I just checked the weather app on my new phone, and there's a big storm heading our way."

"I've driven in rain before," Emma said.

"You win. Be careful. See you tomorrow night," Roy said, then added, "Harry wants us here two hours before the show."

"I can do that."

"Don't feed the cats tomorrow. They perform better when they're hungry."

"Got it," Emma said.

Roy went back on stage and began flirting with Bardot.

Emma whispered to the cats, "We're going to Grammy's house. Trust me. There'll be lots of food."

Cadabra ran her tongue over her lips.

Emma giggled. "And, in the morning, Grammy will make you a great breakfast, too."

She threw her cross-body bag over her shoulder, then wheeled the cart to the hotel exit. Opening the door, she was hit by a blast of hot, humid, late-spring air. A group of tourists were standing nearby. She was glad they ignored her. Usually she was bombarded by curious onlookers wanting to look in at the cats. *That's a first*, she thought. The Siamese had many fans.

She wheeled the cart off the curb onto the paved lot and headed toward the back of the parking lot. She peeked in at the cats. They were spooned together. Cadabra was grooming Abra's head.

"You guys are awfully quiet," she observed. "Quiet before the storm," she kidded.

A loud clap of thunder sounded overhead.

"Oh, no. I think I just jinxed it." Emma began to wheel faster.

Abra whined.

"I know, sweetie. I don't like storms either. I'll try to get us to the car ASAP."

Halfway to the car, the rain started — first a few drops pelted the top of the carrier, then a torrential downpour began.

"Just great," Emma complained, getting drenched. She took off her summer-weight jacket and threw it over the cat carrier. She picked up her pace and ran the luggage cart through rows of parked cars until she found her Toyota Corolla. Hurriedly, she fumbled with her keys, and unlocked the door on the passenger side. She placed the carrier on the seat and secured it with the seat belt.

Emma startled when a strike of lightning hit nearby. Smelling the ozone, she panicked. She quickly collapsed the luggage cart and threw it on the back seat, then ran to the driver's side. Getting in, she said to the cats, "Sorry about this." She fired up the engine, and turned on the windshield wipers, which could barely keep up with the rain.

A second clap of thunder boomed overhead.

The Siamese began shrieking.

Clutching the steering wheel, she turned and looked inside the cat carrier. Quoting a famous Bette Davis line, she said, "Fasten your seatbelts, it's going to be a bumpy night."

Abra pawed the steel-wire door. Cadabra wailed a shrill howl. The Siamese began caterwauling.

"I've got to drive, so I want you two to settle down."

The cats shrilled louder.

Emma drove out of the parking lot and made her way to the highway that would take them to Nyack. The Friday late-afternoon traffic was bumper-to-bumper. The cats continued their incessant, loud yowls.

"Please, calm down. You're making me more nervous than I already am," Emma said uneasily. "I've got things to figure out."

She thought about the other reasons why she was so stressed. She had to find a way to stop Harry from endangering the lives of the cats. She knew going against Harry would get her fired, so she added the quandary of finding a new job to her problem list. She worried about Roy borrowing money from a loan shark. She knew he didn't spend twenty-five grand on moving his new wife from Ohio. She'd worked long enough with him to know he liked to play the slots at the casino. *And, the Mount*

Everest of worries, she thought, *I've fallen in love with the Siamese*.

She said aloud to the cats, "I've got to find a way to keep you. I can't let that jerk Harry hurt you."

The Siamese became quiet, and snuggled up to take a nap.

Once at her grandmother's house, Emma parked in the back of the Victorian, underneath a covered carport. She climbed out, and lifted the cat carrier. Her grandmother, Pearl, met her at the rear door.

"You got lucky. It stopped raining a few minutes ago," Pearl said.

"Hi, Grammy. We're back."

"I see that," Pearl said with a big grin. "Hurry in. I've got a pot roast in the oven with potatoes, onions, and carrots, cooked the way you like it."

"Aw, I love you, Grammy," Emma said fondly. "The cats are stressed from the drive, and the thunderstorm didn't help. I think I'll lock them up in my bedroom."

"Lock them up? My word, let's not make that mistake again. I closed the doors to the rooms with the breakables. They can run all they like. Oh, and while you were gone, I went to the pet store and bought cat food — the premium stuff."

"Oh, that was sweet. They'll love it. They haven't eaten all day, except for the treats Roy gave them."

"Come to the kitchen," Pearl directed, walking through the mudroom to a kitchen with appliances that hadn't been updated since the sixties. She moved over to the gas stove and turned the oven dial off. "How was work today?"

"Roy taught the Siamese a new trick."

"He's the animal trainer, right?"

"Uh, huh, he's very good at his job, but sometimes he can be Mr. Creepy."

"Mr. Creepy? How do you mean?"

"He's like thirty years older than me, but he says these cheesy pick-up lines," Emma said, setting the carrier down. "I get along with him okay, but sometimes his innuendos bother me." She opened the carrier, but the Siamese remained inside. "It's okay, girls. Come on out. We're safe here. No more storm."

The Siamese shifted from side-to-side, then sat down on their haunches.

"I bet they're hungry," Pearl said. "I'll feed them now." She opened a can, scooped out dollops of food, and put it on china plates. "Here, kitty, kitties," she said, placing the dishes on the floor by the refrigerator.

The Siamese sniffed the air, then darted out of the carrier. They raced over to the plates and began eating ravenously. "Raw," Abra said in a muffled voice.

"You're welcome," Pearl laughed. "What's the name of the one that just talked?"

"That's Abra. The other one is Cadabra."

"How can you tell them apart?"

"Abra is a bit smaller than her sister."

"My goodness, they're hungry," Pearl observed.

"Roy says cats are easier to train when they're hungry. When they do a good job or learn something new, he gives them a treat, so it's not like he's starving them."

"Speaking of starving, can you set the table while I take the roast out?"

"Sure, but let me do that. Where are the hot pads?"

"Here," Pearl said, handing them to her.

Emma opened the oven, removed the roast and set it on top of the stove. "Oh, my goodness, Grammy, you've outdone yourself. It smells delicious."

*   *   *

After they finished their meal, Emma rose from the table and took the plates to the sink. "I need to talk to you about something," she said seriously.

"By all means, come back and sit down," Pearl said, concerned. "I know something is bothering you, because usually you're talking my ear off, but tonight, you've hardly said a word."

"I've got a problem at work," Emma began, then recounted the magician's box story to her grandmother. When finished, she asked, "What am I going to do?"

Without skipping a beat, Pearl advised, "Take the cats away from that awful man."

"And, do what, Grammy? Where will I take them? They can't live with me, because I travel all the time."

"Well, that's a no-brainer. Bring them here. I've got plenty of room in this old house for two little stage cats. It's been lonely since my old tom cat died," Pearl said sadly.

"I miss Boots too, but I can't just *take* the cats."

"I'd say it's more like a rescue mission."

"The cats are worth a fortune. Harry's a jerk, but he's not stupid. He'd smell a rat as soon as the cats went missing, and would call the police. I'd be the number-one suspect."

"Let's put our heads together and come up with a plan where *we* wouldn't get caught," Pearl plotted.

"Did you say *we*? I don't want you involved in this."

"Hear me out. Maybe after the performance, I can help."

"And do what?"

"Today, in the pet store, I saw these duffel-style cat carriers for sale. There's a large size that would fit two cats. I could ask my friend Lawrence to help. If you could get us backstage passes, we could wait for the show to be over, then when possible, we'd meet up with you, and transfer the cats from your carrier to ours—"

"Wait, just a second. If you did that, how would I explain to Harry that his professional cat handler misplaced his star performers? The Siamese are the reason why people come to the show, you know that, right?"

"You'll think of something. Lawrence and I will whisk the cats to my car."

"The getaway car?" Emma laughed, not taking her grandmother's plan seriously. "I can picture it now. By the way, who's Lawrence?"

"A guy I met online. We've been dating for a few months now."

"Really?" Emma asked, surprised. "That's great. Why haven't you told me?"

"I guess I wasn't sure how you'd take it. I know how close you were to your grandfather."

"Grandpa passed away a long time ago. I think it's great you're seeing someone, but I don't want my first meeting with your boyfriend to be at the county jail."

"Three partners in crime," Pearl said.

"I'm not sure your snatching the cats is a good idea. I'm pretty much sure the two of you would never make it outside the backstage door. The Siamese would be very loud — that alone would alert hotel security."

"No one is going to pay any mind to a bunch of silver-haired coots. My generation is invisible, didn't you know."

"That's nonsense, Grammy."

"I'll think of something. We've got to rescue those cats before one of them gets hurt."

"It's very sweet of you to want to help, but let me think of a plan — one where I won't end up in the county lockup. Wearing an orange jumpsuit is not going to put me on the cover of a glamour magazine."

"Hee, hee," Pearl giggled.

"Ma-waugh," Cadabra agreed.

"Raw," Abra seconded.

Abra lunged over to Cadabra and playfully bit her on the neck. Cadabra bit her back. This initiated the steeplechase race. The Siamese darted out of the room and thundered up the stairs.

Emma and Pearl roared with laughter.

Chapter Seven

Friday Evening

From the Catskills, Roy took a train to Penn Station, and got on another train to Oyster Bay. Sitting in the back of the LIRR train car, he lamented at how much time it took to get from his apartment to the resort hotel where the performance would be. He thought, *That damn Harry is too cheap to book us rooms to stay at the hotel. Here I am wasting hours to get home.*

He leaned his head back and fell asleep, but didn't sleep for long. A nagging worry woke him up. He took out his cell and called his aunt, who answered on the fourth ring. She wasn't in a good mood.

"How are you, Auntie?" he asked quietly so as to not disturb the other passengers.

"Quite frankly, I'm not very happy with you. We agreed that you would pay rent on the carriage house. You haven't paid me a single dime since you moved here," she complained.

"I'm a little bit strapped for cash right now. I apologize. I was wondering if you could loan me some money."

There was a pause, and then the aunt shrieked into the phone, "Absolutely not. You have a gambling problem. Get help!" She hung up.

Roy arrived at the carriage house, but didn't use his key to the front door. He wanted to avoid running into his aunt at all costs. He didn't want a confrontation with his aunt, who would be sure to complain to his mom. The last thing he wanted was his nosy mother on his back.

He crept up the back stairs to the second story landing, unlocked the door, and headed to the kitchen. Opening the refrigerator door, he grabbed a bottle of beer, twisted the cap off and took a long, hard drink. Then he sat down at the table, and reflected on how he'd really screwed up this time. He had to get the money to pay off his loan-from-hell, or the mob would be after him. He knew he had a serious gambling problem, but he just couldn't stop.

He found his phone and texted his wife to ask when she'd be home. In a few seconds, she answered that she'd stayed later than five o'clock, and a car service was driving her. She'd be home in a few minutes. Earlier in the day, she'd texted that she had gotten a new job. When she finally walked through the door, he hurried to hug her. Holding his wife close, he said, "Jules, I really missed you today. What's cookin', good lookin'?"

"We need to celebrate," Julia said, kicking off her white nurse shoes.

"And why is that?" he asked, kissing her ear.

"My new job is at a mansion outside of Oyster Bay. The couple is fantastic. The wife loves cats, and is so nice, it's unfortunate she has cancer." Julia's voiced trailed off.

"What kind of cancer?"

"She has a rare thyroid cancer."

"Is it treatable?"

Julia shook her head. "From my experience, this kind of cancer is very difficult to treat."

"That's too bad. Sorry to hear that. Wipe that out of your mind. Would you like to have dinner with me?"

"Where?" she asked.

"I've made a reservation at our favorite Italian restaurant on the water."

"I love that idea."

"Oh, before we go, I picked up a playbill for Saturday's performance."

"A playbill? What's that?" Julia inquired.

"It's something the ushers hand out to the audience as they come in. I know how much you love cats. I'm working with a pair of Siamese."

"Siamese?" Julia asked, thrilled. "What kind?"

"Cats," Roy teased.

"No, I meant what kind of Siamese? I used to have a seal-point."

"They're seal-points, but they don't look like your run-of-the-mill Siamese."

"Bite your tongue. Siamese are never run-of-the-mill."

Roy moved to the table and picked up the playbill. He flipped several pages to the page he'd dog-eared. "Take a look. They look exotic, right?"

Julia joined Roy at the table. "Good gravy," she said, aghast.

Roy looked surprised. "What's the matter with you?"

"This cat looks exactly like the one my employer just lost." She pointed at one of the Siamese.

"That's Abra, but trust me, she's not the lady's lost cat."

"I didn't mean lost, I meant to say, the cat died. Mrs. Lincoln — that's my new employer's name — had a life-size portrait painted with the cat."

"Interesting."

"Can I have this playbill to show her on Monday?"

"Sure, why not?"

"Maybe her husband can contact your boss to find out where he bought the Siamese. Then he can go to that breeder, and buy one for his wife," Julia said thoughtfully.

"I thought you said your employer has cancer?" Roy asked, confused.

"Yes, she does, but I think a new cat would help her quality of life."

Roy burst out laughing. "Jules, you said the couple lives in a mansion. I'd call that an excellent quality of life."

Julia affectionately poked her husband on the arm.

"Well, don't get too attached to your patient," he advised.

"What do you mean?"

"I just got word that the next gig is in Vegas."

Julia jaw dropped. "Vegas? We just moved here. I just started a new job."

"I told ya when I married you that in my line of work, I travel. I go where the show is, and Harry said it's going to be in Vegas."

"When? For how long?"

"The Catskills gig ends early September. Don't know the dates, but I figure Harry will be moving the show soon thereafter."

Julia wore a long face. "I guess I should have known this was the deal when I married you. This is why you wouldn't let me bring my cat here because you knew we'd be traveling a lot. Right?"

"Let me wipe that frown off your face," Roy said, kissing Julia on the lips.

Julia forced a smile, then asked, "How was your day?"

"Too long. This commute is killing me. I guess I'm tired, and too hungry to think straight," he said wearily, then switched gears and asked, "Jules, I assume the couple is rich. Are they filthy rich?"

"How would I know? I didn't look in their bank account. Why do you want to know?"

"No particular reason. I'm just curious about the working conditions of my wife."

Julia smiled. "Oh, how sweet. On that note, I'm going to change into something more suitable for a fancy restaurant."

"Wait, just a second. When you show the playbill to Mrs. Lincoln, tell her that Magic Harry is retiring Abra, and for the right price, he'll sell her," he squinted, lying. "He asked me to be the agent in the sale."

Julia looked skeptical. "What? Seriously?"

"Yes, for real. The darn cat has really been messing up in the rehearsals," Roy said. "My boss said he wanted to get rid of her and find another cat that would do a better job."

"Okay, I'll mention it Monday. How much is he asking?"

"Twenty-five thousand dollars."

"Twenty-five thousand dollars," she repeated in disbelief. "That much money for a cat?"

"Not just a cat, but a stage-performing Siamese from a grand champion bloodline. Harry said he has her papers to prove it."

Julia covered her mouth to stifle a laugh. "You're nuts. I hate it when you tease me."

Roy slapped his knee, laughing, "I gotcha on that one. I'm just kidding."

"What time is the reservation?" Julia asked, changing the subject.

Roy looked at his watch. "We've got a half-hour."

"Let's stop this cat chat and get ready."

Roy pulled his wife into an embrace. "I'm crazy about ya, cupcake."

"Ditto, right back at you," Julia answered.

Chapter Eight

Saturday — Opening Night

The Last Act

Emma knelt down beside the empty cat carrier and waited for Abra and Cadabra to finish their set and run off the stage. She opened the carrier's metal gate all the way, and arranged the rumpled cat blanket to cover the bottom.

During the intermission, she'd talked to Harry. He was in a good mood, and seemed to have forgotten their quarrel over the cat-sized magician's box. He even asked her to attend the after-show party in his hotel suite. She declined because she wanted to take the Siamese back to her grandmother's house for the rest of the weekend.

Kneeling by the carrier, she could tell the performance was going well. The roar of the applause and cheers were almost deafening.

At the designated time, Abra ran off the stage first, followed by Cadabra. The cats made a beeline straight for the carrier.

Emma hurriedly shut the door and latched it. "Good girls," she praised in a soft voice.

The audience continued clapping. She thought, *Wow, Magic Harry and Bardot must be getting a standing ovation.*

Emma looked in at the Siamese. "You must have really done a super job because—" She wasn't able to finish her sentence.

Two men came up behind her. One of them hit Emma in the back of the head with something heavy. She blacked out and collapsed on the carrier, which made the cage fall on its side.

The second man asked, "Shouldn't we just kill her? She might have seen us, or something."

"Shut up, Jimmy. Get moving. Dump her in that room over there," he pointed.

"I'm on it, Benny," the loan shark said, picking up Emma and carrying her to the backstage ladies' room.

Benny righted the cat carrier. He dropped a zippered duffel bag next to it. He unzipped it part of the way.

Inside the carrier, Abra stood in front of Cadabra. Her ears were drawn back and laid flat on top of her head. She hissed. Cadabra snarled. Both cats growled ferociously. Cadabra cried, "Mir-yowl, yowl, yowl."

Benny slipped on heavy gloves, reached in, and yanked Abra out by the scruff of her neck. Abra became a thrashing, clawing machine, but her claws and bites were no match for the man's thick gloves. Benny tightened his grip on her neck. Abra dangled in the air, instinctively bringing up her back legs to claw him.

"Keep that up, you little bitch, and I'll kill you."

Jimmy returned. "Stop it. We need her alive."

"Shut up," Benny said. He stuffed Abra in the duffel bag and zipped the bag. Abra continued thrashing inside. The two men ran to the exit and left the hotel. A car pulled up and they jumped in.

Back in the cat carrier, Cadabra collapsed on her side and cried a pitiful "waugh."

Harry and Bardot remained on stage, taking their final bows.

Bardot left the stage before Harry. She wore a blue-sequined bodysuit, with fishnet stockings and high-heeled, strapped shoes. She carried a dozen red roses. She was too caught up in the moment to look where she was going. She stumbled over the cat carrier and came down hard on her knee.

"Ouch," she winced, then stood up and bent over to massage her sore knee.

"Help," someone cried from the ladies' room.

"Who said that?" Bardot asked, looking around.

"Help," the voice said again. "I'm in here."

Bardot moved to the ladies' room, opened the door and found Emma sprawled on the floor.

"What happened to you?" she asked.

"I've been attacked. Get Roy."

"Sugar, I'm going to do more than that." She rushed outside the room and shouted at the top of her lungs, "We need security in here." She waited a few seconds, then shouted again. "Security!"

Roy left his position off-stage, right wing, and made his way to the crossover hallway behind the upstage curtain. He was midway through the hall when he heard Bardot shouting. Because the audience was still clapping, he couldn't tell where the sound was coming from, then Bardot shouted again.

Roy bolted down the hall and rounded the corner. Bardot stood in front of the ladies' room.

"What's going on?" he asked.

"Call 9-1-1. Emma's injured," she said frantically.

"You call it," Roy demanded. "I don't have my cell on me."

"Does it look like I have a pocket for my phone in this get-up?"

"Find a phone. Get going!"

Roy rushed into the ladies' room.

Emma lay on her side in a fetal position. Her hands were clasped behind her head. "Am I bleeding?" she asked.

"No, it doesn't look like it. What happened?"

"Someone hit me on the back of the head."

"In the ladies' room?" Roy asked skeptically.

"No, Roy, not here, but outside," she said weakly. "Are the cats okay?"

"Why? What about the cats?"

"I was with them when I got hit. Someone must have dragged me in here," she gasped.

Bardot returned, wearing a jacket over her skimpy costume. "I went to my dressing room and called an ambulance," she announced. "Emma, is there anything you need?"

"Can you go look for my grandmother in the theater or concession area? She has a pass to come back here, but she hasn't shown up."

"I can do that. What does she look like?" Bardot asked.

"She's got shoulder-length silver hair. Her name is Pearl."

"Wait a sec. I can't go out there in my costume, but I'll ask one of the stagehands to get her," she said, starting to leave.

Roy said, "Hey, Bardot, wait. Stay with Emma until I get back. I've got to check on the cats."

"That's what I meant to tell you," Bardot said in her signature gravelly voice. "One of them is missing."

"Why didn't you tell me that in the first place?" Roy asked angrily.

"Don't you raise your voice to me," Bardot countered.

"Oh, never mind," he said, leaving the room. He ran to the carrier and looked in on Cadabra. He opened the front gate and reached in. He petted her and spoke in a soothing voice, "It's going to be okay. Calm down, little girl."

"Waugh," Cadabra whimpered.

Harry exited the stage and walked over to Roy.

"What's going on here?" he asked gruffly. "Where's Emma?"

"Abra's missing," Roy said, "and Emma—"

Harry interrupted, "Are you freaking kidding me? Call security, then get some stagehands and search the back area. Tell them to check the bird room first. The dang cat is probably in there messing with the pigeons. I'm going to find that incompetent Emma—"

"Harry, stop, Emma has been injured. Someone assaulted her. Bardot called an ambulance; it's on its way."

"So, what does that have to do with my best performer going missing?" Harry asked without empathy.

"I repeat! Someone hit Emma and stole Abra," Roy explained angrily, then backtracked, "I mean Abra got out."

"Got out? Stolen? Make up your mind. Which one is it?"

"I meant she got out."

Harry quickly summed up the situation. "Oh, I get it. Emma's injured?" he doubted. "She's faking. It's all a ploy for her to steal Abra. She's wanted her from day one. I'm calling the police and telling them just that."

"That's ridiculous. She's not faking," Roy protested.

"Bull crap. In the meantime, tell Emma, wherever she is, she's fired. I'll send her check through the mail."

Harry stomped off to his dressing room, shouting "Where's the dang hotel security?"

Roy stood motionless, stunned by Harry's cold behavior. He cursed a few words aloud.

A stagehand ran down the hall.

Roy called to him, "Hey, Bryan, could you do me a favor and take this cat carrier to my dressing room, then round up a couple of guys? Harry wants us to search for a missing cat."

"Sure, but what happened?" the man asked.

"Emma's been hurt. Ambulance is coming. I can't talk right now."

"Okay," the stagehand said, lifting the carrier. Cadabra cried a series of shrieks.

When the EMTs arrived, Roy directed them to Emma.

Bardot brushed by the first EMT. "I've got to find Emma's grandmother," she said as she rushed by.

Emma was sitting up, with her arms by her side. "Roy, are the cats okay?" she asked feebly.

Roy hesitated, then answered, "Cadabra is fine, but Abra escaped from the carrier. Don't worry. I'm sure we'll find her. Just concentrate on getting better."

Emma became agitated and tried to get up. The closest EMT restrained her.

"Miss, you've had a blow to the head," he said. "We want you to be quiet," then to Roy, "Sir, please, go outside. We'll take care of her now."

"Emma, I've got to look for Abra," Roy said, starting to leave.

"Roy, come back. She didn't escape from the carrier — someone stole her."

Roy asked, "Did you see who did it?"

"No," Emma answered, wondering why Roy had asked that question when she'd clearly told him she was hit from behind, then she realized he seemed to be more concerned with Abra's welfare than her own.

"Sir, I'm not going to tell you again. Leave," the EMT said to Roy.

Roy put his hands up defensively. "Okay. Got it!" he said, exiting.

A third EMT wheeled in a gurney.

The EMT that had yelled at Roy, said, "Josh, elevate the backrest to 45 degrees. Her head needs to be elevated."

The man adjusted the head of the gurney.

"Miss, we're going to lift you up. Don't try and sit back on the cot until we place the pillow behind your head."

"Okay," she said.

The two attendants carefully lifted her and placed her on the gurney.

Pearl rushed into the room. "I'm Emma's grandmother. What's going on?"

"Ma'am, we're taking your granddaughter to the ER. She's suffered a possible brain injury."

"Oh, my word."

"Grammy, come closer. I need to tell you something," Emma said.

Pearl walked to the side of the gurney and took Emma's hand.

"Closer than that," Emma said.

Pearl leaned in and put her ear to Emma's lips.

Emma whispered frantically, "Why did your boyfriend hit me in the head? I told you to not go through with your plan."

"We didn't. Security wouldn't let us back here. What happened?"

"Someone stole Abra, but they left Cadabra."

Pearl frowned. "I'm so sorry. We'll talk about this later," then she said to one of the EMTs, "Where are you taking her?"

"To the county regional hospital."

"I don't know where that is. Can I ride in the ambulance?"

"Yes, by all means," he said.

"Bless your heart," she thanked the EMT, then said to Emma, "I need to text Lawrence and tell him what's going on."

"When you find out, could you please tell me, because I don't have a clue," Emma asked, beginning to slur her words.

"No more talking, sunshine," Pearl said.

Chapter Nine

Sunday

Emma's Discharge from the Hospital

A nurse wheeled Emma out of the hospital. Pearl followed, carrying Emma's cross-body bag.

Lawrence, driving Pearl's car, pulled up to the curb and parked. Pearl waved at him from the sidewalk and motioned for him to get out.

The nurse asked Emma, "Do you feel okay to stand up?"

"Yes, I'm fine."

Pearl tapped Emma on the shoulder. "I'll get in on the other side and sit next to you."

"Nurse, I'll help," Lawrence said, coming around the Ford Crown Vic. He took one of Emma's arms. The nurse took Emma's other arm, and between the two of them, they helped Emma get in the backseat. "By the way, I'm Lawrence," he said, introducing himself to Emma.

"Please to meet you," Emma answered.

"Best of luck," the nurse said, rolling the wheelchair back into the hospital.

"Thanks for everything," Emma called after her.

Lawrence climbed back into the driver's seat and put the car in gear. "Where're we heading, ladies?"

Emma asked, "Can you drive to the Catskills Resort Hotel . . . actually to the hotel's parking lot? That's where my car is parked."

Pearl protested. "Emma, you can't drive a car. The ER doctor said you've suffered a mild concussion. He gave me a long list of things you cannot do for a while, and one of them is driving."

"But I can't leave my car in the parking lot. It'll be towed."

Lawrence offered, "Emma, I have no problem driving your car to Pearl's house."

"Thank you so much. I really appreciate it."

"Sounds like a plan," he said, pulling into traffic.

Emma said to Pearl in a low voice, "Well, Grammy, I guess my brief career as a cat thief is over."

"I'm sorry, sunshine."

"Can you explain to me what happened after the show? Why didn't the two of you use your backstage passes?"

"Afterwards, Lawrence and I bumped into an old friend of mine and her husband. We chatted a bit, then I realized everyone had left the theater, so we excused ourselves and headed to the stage door you told us to go to. This hotel security guard was standing in front of the door. He said there had been a security breach in the back and he couldn't honor our passes. I'm not a drinker, but I swear he was three sheets to the wind."

"Just my luck, a drunk security guard. That explains why he wasn't there to prevent me from being attacked."

"I know how much the cats meant to you. Why don't you call Roy and ask him if Abra has been found?"

He sent me a text about an hour ago. Abra is still missing, but Cadabra's okay."

"Where's Cadabra?"

"At the hotel, in a cage," Emma answered sadly. "I can only imagine how miserable she is without her sister."

Pearl became agitated. "We can't leave that poor cat with that monster. We've got to go get her."

"Grammy, that's impossible."

"Why? Surely there's a way."

"Roy mentioned something else in the text."

"What was that?"

"Harry fired me. If I try to come back to the hotel, he's instructed security to remove me."

Pearl sighed. "I'm so sorry, Emma, but there are some horrible bosses out there. Maybe it's good you'll be away from him."

"Yes, it is, especially for his personal safety. I want to kill him."

"Oh, you don't mean that. Did Roy mention anything about the investigation?"

"The police have no suspects, except—"

"Except who?" Pearl asked.

"That good-for-nothing Harry told the police I did it. Can you imagine? I hit *myself* in the back of the head to make it look like a theft."

"He's crazy."

"So, you see, my little plot to rescue the cats and bring them to your house wouldn't have worked out anyway. I'd be busted big time."

"So, you'd planned on cat-napping them after all?"

"Yep."

Pearl began, worried. "When the police showed up last night, and made me leave your room, I didn't know what was going on. I mean, you'd just gotten out of the ER, and taken to an observation room. I thought they could have at least waited until you felt better to interview you."

"The cops were just doing their job. Don't worry, Grammy. After I talked to them, they seemed convinced that I had nothing to do with it."

"Emma, dear, do you have any idea who hit you?"

"Not a clue."

"Let's not worry about it."

"I can't stop worrying about it. I'm an unemployed twenty-something with no job prospects in mind."

"Why don't you go back to school? You can live with me. That would be so much fun?"

"The thought crossed my mind. I've got enough money saved to go to school, that is, enough for a year or two."

"Sounds like a wonderful plan," Pearl said, taking Emma's hand into hers. "NYU is just a hop, skip away," then changed the subject, "Not to sound bossy, but can you do something for me?"

"Yes, of course, what?"

"Later today, if you feel up to it, there's someone I want you to talk to."

"Who?"

"My dear friend, Miriam, belongs to an animal welfare group. You need to report that despicable man."

"Grammy, I have no power to stop him."

"But maybe Miriam's group can."

Lawrence drove into the resort hotel's parking lot. "Emma, where's your car parked?" he asked.

"Drive all the way to the back of the parking lot. It's a blue Toyota Corolla," Emma said, searching her bag for her keys.

Pearl said to Lawrence, "I bet you're exhausted."

"I got some sleep, but let me tell ya about the furniture at the hospital. The sofa was as hard as a rock," he answered.

"I feel terrible you didn't get any sleep," Emma apologized.

"I'd do anything for your grandmother, and that includes you."

"Aw," Pearl said with a gush of gratification. "Lawrence, you're such a doll."

Emma nodded toward Lawrence. "Grammy, you have my seal of approval."

"He's a keeper," Pearl said happily.

Chapter Ten

Monday Morning

Upper West Side of Manhattan

Roland Lincoln instructed his driver to pull in front of the Specialty Top Cats pet store and let him off. "I'm not sure how long this will take," he advised. "Maybe a few minutes, maybe longer. Just drive around the block and find parking where you can. I'll text you when I'm ready."

"Yes, sir," the driver said.

Roland got out of the limo and walked inside the store. He quickly glanced around the room at the individual glassed enclosures full of kittens — all kinds of kittens. He recognized a few of the breeds: Persian, Burmese and Himalayans. A middle-aged woman with short, spiky red hair approached from the back.

"Welcome," she said warmly. "My name is Margaret. How may I help you this morning?"

"I'm looking for a Siamese," Roland said.

"Oh, you're in luck. I have several pedigreed Siamese kittens from a magnificent bloodline. Their mama was a grand champion, having won several award ribbons at cat shows held throughout the United States. Over here," she said, walking over to an enclosure of four kittens: two seal-points, a lilac-point and a blue-point.

"I'm not looking for a kitten. I'm looking for an adult Siamese. A seal-point with a wedge-shaped head—"

"And sapphire blue eyes," the woman finished.

"Yes, exactly. Allow me to introduce myself. My name is Roland Lincoln. My wife and I live out on Long Island. We recently lost our Siamese to cancer."

"I'm sorry to hear that."

Roland continued, "My wife is battling cancer herself. She's mourned the loss of Duchess to the point where, I believe, it has affected her recovery."

"That's very unfortunate. Was Duchess your cat's name?"

"Yes."

"Where do you live on Long Island?"

"Oyster Bay. Can you tell me if you have any adult Siamese, preferably a female? If it's a simple no, I can text my chauffeur to pick me up."

"Chauffeur," the woman said, eyeing Roland curiously, noting that he must have money to have a personal driver. "I do have an adult Siamese cat who just came in. She's a rescue."

"How old is she?" Roland asked.

"She's approximately two-years-old."

"That's perfect," Roland said, thinking about Duchess's age when she died.

"However, allow me to make myself clear. She's a rescue and comes 'as is.'"

"What does that mean? Comes 'as is?'"

"It means I don't know anything about her history — whether or not she's had her shots or even been seen by a veterinarian."

"Okay, I'm good with that," Roland said, pulling out his wallet and extracting a photo of Duchess. "This was my Siamese. Does your rescue look like her?"

Margaret ignored the question, but commented, "Beautiful, exquisite Siamese. Did you buy her from my store?"

Roland shook his head. "No, Duchess came from a Siamese breeder out on the island."

"Before I show you the cat, let me say that I take in specialty breed rescues from different rescue organizations or from individuals. These cats may or may not have health or behavioral issues."

"What kind of behavioral problems?"

"I don't know if you are aware, but many Siamese end up in animal shelters because their owners simply cannot stand their incessant meows."

"My wife and I don't have a problem with that. Duchess had quite a vocabulary," he laughed. "We loved her for it."

"A Siamese rescue came to me yesterday afternoon. I haven't had time to take her to the vet for an examination. She's very upset."

"I'd like to see her."

"Follow me to the back. I'll show her to you."

Roland followed the woman through a parted curtain to a small room with several stainless steel cages in it, stacked on top of each other. In the middle cage, lay a lean, wedge-headed seal-point with deep blue eyes. Roland did a dead stop. "Wow," he said. "Unbelievable."

"Something wrong?" Margaret asked.

"This cat is a dead ringer for my cat Duchess."

"Awww," the Siamese cried in a weak voice.

"Is she sick?" Roland asked, getting closer to the cage. "She sounds hoarse."

"She's in some kind of shock from being brought here. I have no idea where she came from. Sometimes my sources are . . . let me find the right words . . . shady at best, but I don't care because I love cats—"

"How much?" Roland asked, cutting her off.

"I'm not sure I want to sell her. She's obviously from a pedigreed bloodline. I could enter her in a cat show. She's perfect in every regard."

"I'll take her."

"But, sir, I haven't told you my price. Certainly, I'd want to be reimbursed for what I paid for her with a little extra 'finder's fee.'"

"Yes, yes. I'm prepared to pay your fee," Roland said impatiently.

"Well on that note," the woman hesitated, then said, "I'm asking thirty-thousand dollars."

"Fine," Roland said without flinching at the exorbitant price. "I'll have my bank wire you the money. Do you have a cat carrier I can buy? I want to take her right now."

"Sir, before we close the transaction, we must have an understanding. Obviously, this cat is a purebred, but because she's a rescue, I have no way of finding out if she's registered —"

"Registered where?"

"CFA. It's an organization that keeps track of bloodlines of purebred cats."

Roland raised his hand dismissively. "Oh, that doesn't matter. My wife and I don't care if she's registered. So, what's the understanding?"

The woman looked down at the floor, then back up. "You must be very discreet and never tell anyone where you got her. You must never show her in a cat show. She must be an inside cat only."

"Yes, of course. I understand," Roland said, then asked, "Wait a minute. Just a few seconds ago, you said you wanted to show the cat."

"I guess I did. Sorry," the woman said, flustered.

"Is the cat stolen?" Roland asked bluntly, getting more irritated by the second.

"Sir, like I said, she's a rescue. I don't know anything beyond that."

"You don't know the person or persons who brought the Siamese to your store?" Roland asked incredulously.

"Well, yes," the woman said, "but he wishes to remain anonymous."

"Say no more. My wife and I will never tell anyone, that is, if you never tell anyone whom you sold the cat to. Deal?"

"Deal," Margaret smiled. "I'll get a carrier," she said, exiting the room and heading to the front of the store.

Roland called after her, "And, I'll need the routing information for your bank. Plus, a litterbox and cat litter."

"Right-o," Margaret answered.

Roland leaned in and put his finger through the cage. "You darling, precious little girl," he admired. "I'm going to take you to your new home now. I know you'll make my wife so happy, and me, too."

The Siamese got up, stretched, and padded over to the man. She blinked an eye kiss and nuzzled his finger. "Raw," she cried.

Chapter Eleven

Duchess the Second

The chauffeur drove into the Lincolns' circular drive and parked in front of the mansion. He got out and opened the rear door. Roland exited, then leaned in to grab the cardboard cat carrier Margaret had sold him. Inside the carrier, the Siamese crouched on the floor, and peered through one of the small circular openings. She inserted her V-shaped jaw and started to chew around the hole to make it bigger. This was something she'd been working on since they'd left the specialty cat store.

"Okay, little girl," Roland said. "You keep that up and you'll be out of that carrier soon. Let's get you to the house."

"I'll help you with your bags," the chauffeur offered.

"Yes, thanks, Mel. Go ahead and park the car in the garage, and bring the cat stuff to my wife's bedroom."

"Yes, sir."

Roland carried the cat carrier to the house. Margo, the personal assistant, saw him coming up the front steps, and opened the door.

"Good morning, Mr. Lincoln. What do you have there?"

"A surprise present for Olivia."

Margo peeked through the top hole of the carrier and complimented. "What a beautiful Siamese. Mrs. Lincoln will be so happy."

Roland smiled a wide grin, and walked into his wife's bedroom.

Olivia was sitting up on the bed, leaning against the headboard. She had a fleece coverlet draped over her lap. Her new nurse, Julia, sat in a nearby chair.

They both looked up with curious interest when Roland walked in.

Olivia said excitedly, "Roe, darling, did you bring me a cat?"

Roland set the carrier on the foot of the bed, undid the top, reached in and pulled out the Siamese.

"Oh—oh—oh," Olivia cried happily. She squeezed her eyes shut in disbelief, then opened them. She stretched her arms out. "Duchess, come to me."

Roland placed the Siamese on his wife's lap.

Olivia drew the cat near and hugged it. She tenderly kissed the Siamese on the head. Happy tears fell from her eyes. "Roe, she looks so much like Duchess," then she digressed, "I assume she's a she." She laughed.

"Yes, dear," he said affectionately. "She's a girl."

"Where did you find her?"

"A cat store on the upper west side."

"What's her name?"

"Olivia, she's a rescue. The woman who sold her to me said she didn't know—"

"We'll call her Duchess the Second."

"Raw," the Siamese cried, purring. "Raw. Raw."

While Roland and Olivia were discussing the new cat on the block, Julia stooped down and drew the playbill out of her purse. She turned to the dog-eared page with Abra's and Cadabra's stage picture. She studied the photo, then looked at the Siamese now called Duchess. Her face dropped.

"Julia, what do you think of us calling our new cat, Duchess? Roland asked, moving over.

Julia stuffed the playbill back into her purse. She composed herself, and smiled warmly, "I think it's a wonderful name. Congratulations!"

Olivia asked, "Julia, can you take our picture?"

"Yes, of course. Group photo of mom and dad with their new fur-child."

Roland handed his cell phone to Julia. He sat down next to Olivia on the bed. Duchess curled up on Olivia's lap and looked directly at the camera. Julia took the photo, then passed the phone back to him.

"It's a very sweet picture," she said.

There was a knock at the door, and the chauffeur, Mel, came in. He was holding a litterbox. "Where do you want me to put it?" he asked.

"Over there in the corner," Olivia instructed.

Julia took this opportunity to walk out of the room. She moved down the long hall toward the formal dining room, opened the French doors, and walked in. She yanked her cell phone out of her pocket and texted Roy. "What time are you getting home? I need to speak to you. It's urgent!"

Julia sat down on an art deco chair and waited for Roy's answer. After fifteen minutes of anticipating a text that didn't come, Julia left the dining room and headed back to Olivia's bedroom. She was livid, but she had to get out of her mood and not show the Lincolns how angry she was. She thought, *I don't know what's going on, but I think Roy had something to do with this.*

Chapter Twelve

Monday Afternoon/The Show Must Go On

Hocus-Pocus Rehearsal

Sarah Goode, the new cat wrangler, wrestled the cat carrier to the center of the stage. Her purple-streaked hair was cut in a shaggy style. She was short and very slender.

Inside the carrier, a Siamese was having a royal cat fit. Cadabra lay on her back and kicked the top of the plastic cage. She shrieked like a banshee. "Waugh," the Siamese protested.

"Cut it out," Sarah shouted at the cat. "I can't take it. Shut up right now," she said, setting the carrier down, a little too hard, on the floor. She jiggled the front metal gate for emphasis. "I mean it!"

Roy rushed over. "Sarah, that's not the way to communicate with a cat. You must have a quiet voice. You're upsetting Cadabra by being angry. She's already upset by what happened the other night."

"Oh, that's ridiculous. You act like the cat's in mourning or something. Do your own job! I know what I'm doing," the woman answered haughtily.

Magic Harry strode in, carrying a large cardboard box. "Is there a problem here? I thought I heard yelling."

Sarah smiled a toothy grin. "Hello, Harry. How are you?" she asked in a sugary voice.

"Just fine, thank you," Harry answered. "Roy, are we ready?"

"Ready for what?" the animal trainer asked.

Harry placed the box on the floor. "Warren just delivered this. It's a cat-sized magician's box. I sent you an email about it yesterday. Today, I want you to train Cadabra to be comfortable getting in and out of it."

"I read it, but my question is, how is she going to be comfortable with her hind legs strapped down?" Roy asked, annoyed.

Harry threw him a dirty look. "You're the animal trainer. You do your job, and I'll do mine."

"I was just telling him that," Sarah shot off.

Harry bent over, reached inside the cardboard box, and lifted out the magician's box and placed it on the trick table. He clamped the circular saw's base to back of the table, ran his fingers over the rubber retractable blade, then plugged the saw into an outlet underneath the table. He picked up the magician's box, lined up the tracks on the bottom of the box with the saw blade, and secured the box to the blade. Once the two pieces were joined, he raised a padded bar that would lower over the cat's back legs. "Okay, Sarah, let Cadabra out," the magician said.

"Wait! Harry, excuse me, one second," Roy requested. "Sarah, did you bring my target stick?"

"Your target stick?" she asked, with one eyebrow up in confusion. "I don't know what that is, but here's a clicker." She handed a clicker to Roy.

Roy muttered, "And you claim to know what you're doing?"

"I heard that," she said.

"Did you bring the canned tuna treats?"

"No," she said, with one hand on her hip. "I brought dry treats I bought at the pet store."

"But, Cadabra doesn't like the dry treats," Roy grumbled.

Harry blurted. "Children, play nice. Sarah, when Roy asks you something, don't give him any lip. Roy, my show isn't about what the dang cat likes. Now, let's get on with it."

Sarah gave a smug smile and handed a few treats to Roy.

One of the doors at the back of the theater opened, then closed. A stately-looking, white-haired woman in her seventies found a seat and sat down. Harry, Roy and Sarah were too far away to notice.

Roy moved to the trick table and used his finger to tap on the box. He gestured to Sarah to open the cat carrier's door.

Sarah opened it wide. Inside, the Siamese didn't budge.

Roy clicked his clicker. "Cadabra, here," he instructed.

The Siamese stretched, slowly walked out of the carrier, sauntered over, and sprang to the table.

Roy gave her a treat and praised, "Good girl."

Cadabra scrunched up her nose in disgust and spit the treat out. It bounced on the floor, then rolled under the table.

Roy picked the Siamese up and cradled her like a baby. He gently placed her in the magician's box.

Cadabra panicked. She used her hind legs to launch out of the device. She soared off the table and ran toward the carrier.

"Oh, no, you don't," Sarah said, shutting the carrier's gate.

Cadabra catapulted off the closed cat carrier, and darted to the left wing.

Sarah was in quick pursuit. "Got you," she said, tackling the cat.

"Waugh," Cadabra wailed.

Harry interjected in a booming voice, "That's a fine kettle of fish. Roy, start over."

Roy suggested to Harry, "Perhaps, initially, Cadabra would do better if it was just me here. No offence, boss, but your voice is rather loud."

"Loud is it? Need I remind you that I'm the star of this show, and I determine the loudness of my voice. You just work for me," Harry said angrily. "Call the cat back, and I'll put her in the box." Harry returned behind the trick table.

Roy instructed, "Sarah, put Cadabra back in her carrier."

The new cat wrangler did what she was told.

Roy clicked his clicker and tapped on the magician's box. "Cadabra, back!"

Sarah opened the gate.

The Siamese launched out of the carrier. At breakneck speed she dashed toward the right wing, spun her back legs on the highly polished floor, then darted to the left wing. She bulleted all over the stage, from left-to-right, back-to-front.

Harry, Sarah and Roy chased her.

Harry yelled at Roy. "For crying out loud, do something."

Upstage, Cadabra leaped on the velvet curtains, and began to climb.

Roy rushed over. "I got her," he announced. He gently grabbed Cadabra's middle, but the Siamese further dug her claws into the heavy fabric. "Come on, my little girlfriend," he cooed. He unhooked one paw and reached over to unhook the other. Cadabra grabbed the curtain with the paw he'd just unhooked.

Harry rushed over and forcibly yanked the cat off the stage curtain. The Siamese yelped in pain. One of her front claws had broken to the quick and was now bleeding.

Harry was oblivious to the injury. He flipped Cadabra over on her back and pushed her into the box. He barked at Roy, "Pull the bar over her legs."

Cadabra became a wild animal. She struggled to get free from Harry, succeeded, leaped off the table, and ran to the edge of the stage. There she stopped in sudden surprise.

A woman was marching down the aisle, carrying a clipboard.

Harry noticed the woman and shouted, "You're not supposed to be here. This is a closed rehearsal."

The woman walked up to the stage, tucked the clipboard under her arm, and pulled Cadabra off the stage. She held the upset Siamese and petted her. "There now, sugar pop. It's okay, precious." Cadabra collapsed against her and began to purr loudly.

Harry repeated, "Put my cat down and get out!"

"My name is Miriam Foster. I'm a case worker for the state's animal advocacy organization," she said, addressing Harry. "We've received a complaint that you intend to use a dangerous device in your show, and the device could seriously injure an animal."

"Who complained about me?" Harry asked. "Was it Emma Thomas? I fired Emma for dereliction of duty."

Miriam pointed at the magician's box on the trick table. "Is that the device you intend to use?" she asked.

"That's none of your business," Harry said arrogantly.

The woman shot him a cold look. "Actually, it *is* my business. And if you make the wrong move, it's the District Attorney's business. I have the power to close down your show if you insist on using a feline or any other animal to perform such a dangerous trick."

"Says who?" Harry asked. His face reddened with anger.

"There are laws that protect animals. You need to stop what you're doing or face the consequences in court."

Harry waved his hand dismissively. "Are you implying that I'm breaking the law? I've always treated my animals with the utmost of respect."

"I beg to differ," the woman said. She kissed Cadabra on the top of the cat's head and set the Siamese back down on stage.

Cadabra limped to her cat carrier and leaned against it. She sat down on her haunches and began to lick her bloodied claw.

Miriam unclipped a page from her clipboard. "Here's a 'cease and desist' notice. I've delivered one to the owner of this hotel, and here's your copy. To make sure you comply, I will be here at your next performance."

Harry realized the gravity of the situation and lightened up. "Okay, I'm clear."

"Mr. DeSutter, now that I've talked to you in an official capacity, I'll speak to you as a bona fide cat lady. If I had my way, I'd shut your show down permanently. How dare you yank that cat off of the curtains like that? You're such a cruel man, you didn't even notice you'd hurt her claw. Best take care of it," Miriam said, turning on her heels and taking long strides up the aisle to the exit door.

Harry yelled after her, "Who do you think you are?"

Miriam stopped and shouted, "I'm the one holding the clipboard!"

Once he was out of Miriam's earshot, Harry's anger returned. He yelled at Sarah, "Put the dang cat in the carrier, you moron."

"Oh, yes. I'm sorry," Sarah apologized. She snatched Cadabra and roughly threw her in the cage.

"Waugh," Cadabra cried, hitting the side, which made the carrier tip.

Roy ran to the carrier and checked on the Siamese. He gave Sarah an angry look. "If you EVER throw her in like that again, I'll break your neck."

Sarah ran to Harry's side. "He threatened me."

"Sarah," Harry shouted. "What are you still doing here? Take the cat to my dressing room, and while you're there, check out her paw."

"Consider it done," Sarah said, grabbing the cat carrier handle. She lifted the cage and clumped off the stage.

Roy asked, "Well, boss, since you can't use the magician's box, what's your backup plan?"

Harry belted out a laugh. "Backup plan?" he asked incredulously.

Roy looked confused. "The animal advocacy woman just said—"

Harry shook his head. "She's ridiculous. The show must go on."

Roy was quiet for a moment, then said apprehensively, "I can't train Cadabra to do this trick. I might have been able to train Abra, but I know this as a fact, Cadabra will never stand for anyone to strap her hind legs down."

"Boring . . . boring . . . boring. You're like a stuck record. I simply don't have the patience for your whining about Cadabra," Harry complained, then paused briefly. He added, "Roy, I want you to do something for me. Find the nearest animal shelter."

"Surely you don't want me to take Cadabra to an animal shelter?" Roy asked in a shocked voice.

"No, you idiot. I want you to buy, adopt, or whatever the hell those places do, and bring back a cat you *can* train. I've spent a lot of money on this magician's box, and I'm not going to go in debt because *you* can't do your job."

Roy defended himself. "I'm pretty much sure I'm not going to find a Siamese replacement that looks like Cadabra at a shelter."

"The cat doesn't have to be a Siamese."

"Okay, fine. In the meantime, what about Cadabra? What's going to happen to her?"

"She's been screwing up. It's obvious that she can't perform without Abra. I'm retiring her."

"Screwing up? Retiring her? It hasn't even been forty-eight hours since Abra went missing. Can't you give her a little more time?"

"She goes," Harry stated firmly.

"I got a text from Emma yesterday. She's out of the hospital. I know she'd really take good care of her."

Harry scoffed. "Like she's taking care of Abra right now."

"Emma did *not* steal Abra. She's devastated that Abra is still missing."

"Forget about Emma. I wouldn't give her the time of day. If it wasn't for her incompetence, Abra would be with us right now. Case closed. Off you go. Find me a cat you can work with."

"Unbelievable," Roy said, leaving the stage.

"What's unbelievable?" Harry fumed.

Roy stopped and faced Harry. "Listen to me. It would be a bad idea to continue with the magician's box. That advocacy woman could cause you a lot of grief. Think about it. She could go straight to the D.A. or the newspapers. Do you really want negative press right now?"

Harry thought for a moment, then said, "Yeah, you're right. We'll not use the box here."

"That's a relief," Roy said.

"I'll introduce it in Vegas. That will give you time to start training the new cat."

Roy shook his head in shock. "There are animal welfare advocates everywhere."

"Disappear! Get out of my sight," Harry said, heading to his dressing room.

Chapter Thirteen

Monday Evening

Oyster Bay Carriage House

Home of Roy and Julia

When Julia got home from work, she was fuming. All she could think about was confronting Roy. She paced the living room floor. She checked the front window a dozen times, looking for her husband, who was hours late. She was spitting nails. She was so angry at Roy, she was afraid of what she might do to him. When she heard the key turn in the lock, she rushed over to the door.

Roy came in. "What's the matter with you?" he asked with a shocked expression. "You look like you're going to blow a gasket."

Julia thrust the playbill into his chest. "What's the meaning of this?"

"What's ailing you, cupcake?"

"My employers just bought a Siamese that looks identical to this cat in the playbill . . . you know . . . the one that disappeared after Saturday's performance."

"So? A Siamese is a Siamese." He walked to the refrigerator, yanked out a beer, and twisted off the top. "Want one?" he offered. He took a long swig.

She shook her head. "Oh, come on, Roy. I'm not stupid. You weren't messing with me the other night. You knew that cat was going to go missing. Did you steal it and sell it to that pet store on the upper west side?"

"Have you lost your mind? What pet store?"

"I don't know the name of it, but some pet store. Mr. Lincoln said that's where he bought the cat."

"You're not making any sense. Why would I steal the star of the show?"

Julia sat down hard on the sofa. "I've a mind to call the police and tell them where the cat is."

Roy became defensive. He moved over and joined his wife on the sofa. "I wouldn't do that if I were you," he said with an ominous tone.

Julia mouth dropped. She looked hard at his face, then began to cry. "Why? Why did you do it? You could go to jail."

Roy put his arm around her.

She shook it off and got up. "Get your hands off me — you thief!" she shouted.

"Now wait just a minute," Roy said cautiously. "Somehow you've got it in your head that I was the one who stole Abra. That's nuts. I wasn't anywhere near the cat carrier when she was stolen. I was on the other side of the stage."

"Liar," she accused. "I might have believed you, if you hadn't told me that story the other night."

"What story? You're not making any sense."

"Don't try and gaslight me! I'm making perfect sense. When I told you the Lincolns had a Siamese that looked just like one of Magic Harry's cats, you didn't respond the way you should have."

"How was I supposed to respond, Dr. Freud?" Roy quizzed in a mocking tone.

"The normal person would have said something like 'that's cool' or 'look at the resemblance,' but no, not you."

"What's your point?"

"Instead, you wanted to know if the Lincolns had money, so . . . so . . . you could sell them a Siamese that looked like their dead cat. You even said Harry wanted twenty-five-thousand dollars for the Siamese, and that he authorized you to sell it."

"I was just messing with you."

"Really, maybe I should go online and look at our checking account to see if we have twenty-five grand in it."

"Be my guest. What's stopping you?"

"Maybe I should ask Harry if he was in cahoots with you."

"Go ahead. I'm sure he'd love to talk to you," Roy answered sarcastically. "The guy's a jerk."

"It makes me sick to think that you assaulted poor Emma just to get the Siamese."

"I'm innocent," Roy said, throwing his hands up. "The police interviewed me. I told them my side of the story. They went on and interviewed everyone else connected to the show. No one knows what happened to the cat. No one knows who struck Emma."

"You're ridiculous," Julia said, disgusted.

"Jules, I feel awful about this. I really liked Abra. She was a sweetheart. Emma is my friend. The thought that she could have been seriously injured . . . I can't even think about it."

Julia took a deep breath. "Tell me again, so I get it straight, why was Emma injured?"

"I made a bad decision to not be with the cats when they left the stage. I should have been there. Maybe then Emma wouldn't have been hurt."

"That's another thing. All day I texted you about Emma. You never once returned my texts about her. Is she out of the hospital?"

"I thought I told you yesterday. Emma was released and is staying with her grandmother in Nyack."

"You didn't tell me anything," Julia huffed.

"Calm down. Emma suffered a mild concussion. If it's any consolation, I've had the worst day. I didn't answer your texts because Harry already had a replacement for Emma. I had to micro-manage everything she did. She's a nasty woman, and I can't stand her. Plus, Harry had me running a bunch of errands for him."

"You said replacement. Isn't Emma coming back to the show?"

"No, my love, Harry fired her."

"You've got to be kidding me," Julia said, shocked.

"What can I say? Magic Harry is a truly amazing magician who has the ability to make his friends and employees disappear."

"And a cat," Julia muttered, then walked to the dining room sideboard and poured herself a glass of wine. Sipping the wine, she rejoined Roy on the couch.

The couple was quiet for a moment, then Roy said, "I'm on pins and needles around Harry. He's unpredictable. He could fire me any minute, and then you'd have an unemployed husband. Do you know how hard it would be for me to find another animal trainer job? They don't grow on trees."

"No, I don't want that to happen," Julia answered, starting to calm down.

"Are the Lincolns happy with their new cat?"

"Yes," Julia said. "They absolutely adore her."

Roy pulled her near. "So, there you have it. Are you still going to call the police?"

Julia shook her head. "No, I'm beginning to believe you."

"Beginning to believe me? What more can I say to convince you I didn't do it?" Roy asked adamantly.

"I guess I should have put two-and-two together. I can't think of any reputable pet store taking in—"

"A stolen cat," Roy finished. "Besides the Catskills is a heck of a ways from the upper west side."

"Of course, it is," she said, forcing a smile.

"I think it's obvious what you should do." He gulped down the rest of his beer, and set the empty bottle on the end table.

"What's that?" she asked, looking into his piercing gray eyes.

"Love me as I do you," he said gently.

She buried her face in his chest. "Oh, Roy, I don't want this to come between us."

Roy kissed her on the top of her head.

Julia pulled back and looked hard at Roy. "What are the odds that the Lincolns bought a cat that looks just like Abra?"

"It's clearly a coincidence," Roy explained. "Now, end of conversation. Let's go out to eat. I'm starving."

Julia studied Roy's face. She became angry again. "Roy, if I catch you out in another lie, I swear I will leave you. Got it?" she threatened.

"I'll never lie to you," Roy answered, squinting.

Julia rose from the couch and headed to the bedroom. "Order take-out for yourself. I'm not hungry," she said in a sad voice.

"Fine," Roy said, clicking on the TV. "Whatever."

Chapter Fourteen

Two Weeks Later

Julia used her key to let herself into the Lincoln's home, and then walked to Olivia's bedroom. She found Olivia sitting in a wheelchair positioned in front of the window. Nearby, the new Duchess stood tall on the windowsill. The Siamese swiveled her ears in the nurse's direction.

"Good morning, Olivia," Julia greeted, then asked, worried. "Why are you sitting in a wheelchair?"

"Last week's chemo did a number on me. I feel really weak. Roe thought it would be a good idea for me to sit in a wheelchair today, so it would be easier to take me back to the infusion center."

Julia rolled her nurse's bag over and parked it by the chair next to Olivia. She set her handbag on the floor. "Do you think I should call the Center and give them the heads up that you might be coming?"

"Thanks, but I don't think it will come to that. Roe just worries about me."

"I can understand. He's a great guy, but then again, I reckon you know that. Have you had breakfast?" she asked.

"I'm feeling nauseous."

"I'll get you some saltines." Julia reached inside her nurse's bag and pulled out a couple of individually-wrapped crackers. She opened one and handed it to Olivia.

Olivia continued, "I'm also a little tired. I didn't get much sleep last night."

"Why is that?" Julia asked.

"Duchess kept us up. She paced the floor and cried the most dreadful meows. Roland and I took turns holding her. She's been so miserable. It's almost if she's mourning the loss of someone."

"Or another cat," Julia added. "Do you want me to make an appointment with a veterinarian?"

"Ah, no . . . no . . . no need to do that," Olivia answered abruptly. "Roe is having someone come to the house this evening."

"That works."

"Raw," Duchess cried, springing down. With one fluid movement, she hopped onto Olivia's lap.

Olivia kissed the Siamese on her neck. "I love you so much, Duchess. I'm so glad Roe found you." The Siamese stretched up and affectionately tapped Olivia on the cheek.

"I had a rescue once," Julia began. "He was a ginger cat and in terrible health. He was emaciated, and practically starving to death. For the first few days, he was so upset; he huddled in a corner and wouldn't let me pet him. The Lord only knows what he'd been through before I got him."

"What was his story?"

"I'll never know. He was a stray. I found him living in a large drain pipe by my house. He was very skittish of other people, but he adored me."

"Is he still alive?"

Julia frowned. "No, he went to the rainbow bridge a long time ago."

"I take it he came out of his depression."

149

"Yes, in time. Duchess will, too. I'm sure of it."

"Thank you, Julia, for all you do," Olivia said appreciatively. "You're the best."

Julia smiled, and walked to the marble-topped chest where Olivia's medicines were stored. She opened several bottles and extracted the correct pills, then she placed them in a paper pill cup. She poured water into a nearby glass, but instead of returning to Olivia, she stood staring at the wall. Tears pooled in her eyes. She had news to tell Olivia. She didn't know how to drop the bomb.

"Is everything okay over there?" Olivia asked, breaking Julia's depressed chain of thought.

"Oh, yes. Just a second," she said, returning.

"Dear, why are you crying?" Olivia asked softly.

"Oh, it's nothing. Here take your pills," Julia said, placing the pill container in Olivia's hand, then handing her the glass of water.

Olivia popped the pills in her mouth and swallowed. She handed the glass back to Julia. "Why are you upset?"

Julia sat down and faced Olivia. "My Mama raised me to never tell a lie. There's something I need to talk to you about."

"You're not quitting, are you?" Olivia asked, very alarmed.

"I'm not quitting my job. I'm quitting my husband."

"Why? You're newlyweds. What on earth has happened?"

"I won't mince words. My husband is a compulsive liar. I just found out that he also has a serious gambling problem."

"How did you find out?"

"His aunt told me. She waited until now to tell me. Gee, thanks, Penelope."

"Have you talked things over with your husband?"

"Why bother? My husband is a master at his craft. You can't believe a word that comes out of his mouth."

Duchess leaped to the floor, hurried over to Julia, and began sniffing the air.

"Duchess, come here?" Olivia asked in a sweet voice.

"See, even your cat can smell my lying husband."

Duchess began clawing Julia's purse, then she hissed.

"Stop it, Duchess. Come here, right this minute."

Duchess collapsed on her side and began kangaroo-kicking the bag.

Julia leaned down and tried to take the purse, but Duchess growled.

"Whoa, I'm sorry, Duchess, but I think you've killed it," Julia said.

Duchess gave one last kick, and returned to Olivia's lap.

"What was that all about?" Olivia asked the Siamese, then to Julia. "I apologize for Duchess's behavior. Did she damage your bag? Where did you get it? I'll buy you another one."

"My husband, Roy, gave it to me last night," Julia said sadly, then added, "That was before he told me he made an appointment with an attorney."

"An attorney? Why? That is, if you don't mind my asking."

"We have to declare bankruptcy."

"Bankruptcy, but you both work? That doesn't make any sense."

"Actually, it makes perfect sense for Roy. When we got married, we opened joint checking and savings accounts. It was a bad idea."

"How is that a bad idea? I thought that was the thing to do. Roland and I did."

"I closed my savings account in Ohio and had my money transferred to the new account with Roy. Last night, when I got home, I received a letter from the new bank . . . a bank statement. There were zero dollars in our savings account." Julia's eyes narrowed in anger.

"Did you call the bank? It could be a clerical error."

"I wish it were that simple. No, my husband withdrew the money. When I confronted him, he promised he'd put the money back in the account as soon as he could."

"Julia, I can't help but notice. This sounds like a scene out of that Stephen King movie, *Dolores Claiborne.*"

"Exactly, but instead of my husband going to the bank and closing out an account that was solely in my name, Roy legally withdrew the money, which by the way, I'd stupidly deposited in our joint-savings account."

"Did you hit him in the head with a rolling pin?" Olivia asked, making another reference to the movie.

"No, I didn't, but if we'd been standing by an abandoned well, I might have pushed him into it," Julia said bitterly.

"I'm sorry I made such an insensitive comparison to your situation and a scene in the movie."

"It's okay. My feelings weren't hurt. I'm a tough old bird."

"I wouldn't call you old," Olivia commented, then asked, "Don't take this the wrong way, but do you need money? I can loan you some."

"No . . . no, I didn't mean to imply that I want money from you. I have enough to get me by. Thanks so much for offering. You're very kind."

"Okay, but my offer stands. Whenever you need money, I've got you covered. Getting back to last night, what happened after your husband said he'd pay you back?"

"We had a big argument. I stormed out of the room and told him to sleep on the couch. This morning I told him I wanted a divorce. He packed his bags, called a car service, and left for Kennedy Airport."

"Kennedy Airport? Where's he going?"

"Nevada. That's where the next gig is. Magic Harry is moving his show to Vegas."

"My brain's a little foggy this morning. If Roy is in Vegas, how can the two of you meet with an attorney?"

"I'm seeing the attorney about the bankruptcy. I'm also going to ask him to start divorce proceedings."

"Julia, dear, I'm so sorry to hear this. No wonder you're upset. What are you going to do?"

"Roy's aunt said I could stay at the carriage house for a week, but after that I'd have to move. I'm sorry, Olivia, but I have no choice. I'm moving back to Ohio to live with my mom until I can get back on my feet."

"Wait, Julia, but you do have a choice. Let's talk this through. You can move in with us. I have a guest suite on the third floor. I rarely have overnight guests. It would be perfect for you. You could even send for your cat."

"How kind of you to remember I have a cat," Julia said sweetly, then shook her head, "But— "

"No, I won't hear it. I'd be so happy if you'd say yes."

Julia thought for a moment, then said, "I insist on paying rent."

"If that makes you feel better about living here, then so be it. We can talk to Roe about it when he gets back from the city."

"Thank you so much," Julia said, pulling a tissue out of her bag and drying her eyes.

"Now, that we have that problem solved, could you please wheel me to the theater room. Roe bought me a movie for us to watch."

"What movie is it?"

"I forget the name, but it's about two dogs and a cat that take a long journey in the wilderness and end up—"

Julia finished, "*The Incredible Journey*, a Disney movie made in the '60s."

Olivia laughed. "Very good," she said, then to Duchess, "You'll like it. It's got a Siamese in it."

Duchess leaned in and purred, "Raw."

Chapter Fifteen

Vet Clinic, Erie, Indiana

Dr. Sonny opened the door to the patient-examining room and walked in. "I've got Abra's blood test results," he announced. He moved to his computer, clicked the mouse, and pulled up a screen. Katherine and Jake stood behind the stainless-steel examining table, next to the Siamese.

Abra was lying on her side, with a baby blanket covering her up to her chin. She got up, did a full stretch, then walked over to Katherine. Katherine drew her close and cuddled against her. The Siamese began to purr loudly.

"Ah, sweet girl. Are you going to be okay?"

Dr. Sonny explained, "For an eleven-year-old, her blood work is perfect. She's dehydrated, so I want to give her fluids."

"If her bloodwork is okay, then what's wrong with her?" Katherine asked anxiously.

"I'm not sure what caused her collapse. A cat can have an epileptic seizure for various reasons. They can occur spontaneously with no apparent cause. I'm not one-hundred percent sure that Abra had a seizure."

"If she does have another episode, what should we do?" Katherine asked nervously.

"First of all, don't touch her. I know, Katz, you'd want to, and Jake, you too, but clear away obstacles from her. When she's seizing, essentially just leave her alone. When the seizing is over, bring her in and I'll run more tests."

"It wasn't like she was seizing," Katherine answered.

"I was holding her," Jake said. "Her body went limp in my arms. It's more like she fainted."

Katherine agreed. "That's exactly what happened. Abra's body didn't convulse or go rigid. She fainted."

"Sometimes a cat with heart problems can faint, but I've listened to her heart, and it sounds normal."

"I'm relieved to hear that," Katherine said.

"It's possible Abra had an anxiety attack. Katz, what were you doing right before she collapsed?" Dr. Sonny asked.

"I was reading to Jake a newspaper article from the *Times*."

"Is there anything in that article that could have triggered this?" the vet asked.

"Well, as a matter of fact, there was," Katherine said, then hesitated to continue. She didn't want to divulge too much information about the uniqueness of Scout and Abra to the vet.

"What Katz is trying to say is that when she said the name of Abra's previous owner, our little girl fainted."

Katherine nudged Jake in the arm to make him stop talking.

Dr. Sonny noticed the gesture. "Cats are very sensitive creatures and very much in tune with our emotions," he explained. "Perhaps, Abra sensed that *you* were upset by something, and she reacted accordingly."

Katherine explained, "I wasn't really upset. I did get a little excited when I discovered Abra's former owner was being charged with insurance fraud. I mentioned his name several times. Abra didn't seem to react, but I had my back to her."

Jake added, "While I was holding her, she appeared to be listening to every word Katz said. It was almost like she remembered something bad that happened to her in the past—"

"When she was in this person's care," Katherine finished. "That's when she passed out."

Dr. Sonny shook his head. "I don't believe a cat's memory is sophisticated enough to recall past events. Don't get me wrong. Abra is very smart. I'd say that if there was an IQ test for felines, she'd score very high. But, for her to recognize a name and associate that name with a past event, I don't think that's possible. Clearly, I haven't read any studies on this. But, Katz and Jake, there's a tendency to attribute human traits, emotions or intentions to animals.

Let see . . . if I remember the word for it," he said, thinking. "Oh, yes, anthropomorphism."

Jake replied. "In other words, humanizing animal behavior."

Dr. Sonny nodded.

Katherine petted Abra on the head. "Okay, I got that, but can we conduct an experiment?"

"What kind of experiment?" the vet asked.

"I'll say the previous owner's name, and we'll observe Abra's reaction."

Jake touched Katherine on the shoulder. "Do you really think this is a good idea? What if she faints again?"

"Jake, you know I wouldn't do anything to harm one of our precious cats, but I want to rule out Abra having epilepsy."

"I'm not so sure about the scientific authenticity of this experiment," Dr. Sonny began. "I'm banking that Abra has already sensed your emotion."

"I promise to remain calm," Katherine said, taking a deep breath.

"Go for it," Jake said.

Katherine picked up Abra and set her down in the middle of the table. Abra stretched up to full height, and sat back on her haunches.

"Abra, Magic Harry! Harry DeSutter!" Katherine said.

Recognizing the name, Abra flattened her ears against her head, bared her fangs, and cried a deep, throaty growl.

Jake spoke up, "Well, Doc, I guess you can rule out seizures."

Katherine spoke to Abra in a soothing voice. "Sweet girl, I'm so sorry I had to do that."

The Siamese moved to Katherine and leaned against her. She began to purr.

"That's one for the veterinary quarterly journal," Dr. Sonny remarked.

Katherine said, "Can we take her home now?"

The vet shook his head. "I'd like to keep her here for observation. I'll give her the fluids she needs. We close at six. You can pick her up then."

Jake put his arm around Katherine. "I think it's for the best."

Katherine answered in a low voice. "Scout's not going to be happy when we don't bring her sister home."

"She's in safe hands," Dr. Sonny assured. He wrapped the Siamese in the baby blanket, like a feline burrito, and carried her out of the room.

"That's our cue to leave," Jake said. He took Katherine by the arm and led her out of the clinic. They didn't speak until Jake drove his Jeep out of the parking lot.

"Katz, let's not mention Magic Harry's name again."

"Trust me. I won't *ever*," she said with emphasis.

"Are you hungry? Do you want to stop at the diner for breakfast?"

"Is it okay if we just go home?"

"Yes, of course, Sweet Pea. So far, today has been a bummed-out kind of day," he said.

"I don't agree with Dr. Sonny's comment that cats are not sophisticated enough to recall past events."

"I don't, either."

"Remember when Scout and Abra were reunited?"

"Yeah, in your hotel room in Chicago."

"When we put them together, they remembered each other. If they'd forgotten, there would have been a whole lot of hissing going on."

"Oh, I remember," Jake agreed. "They instantly recognized each other."

"Geez, if they didn't, Scout wouldn't have started grooming Abra's head."

They rode for several miles in silence, then Katherine said in a soft voice, "I wish we were back in the pink mansion."

"That's not possible. The attic renovation isn't finished yet," Jake said, turning on to Alexander Street, and heading to the guest house.

"I think our moving around from house-to-house has upset our cats. Do you think Abra is more stressed than the other cats?"

Jake shook his head. "No, I don't think so. She's always been hyperactive. However, I do know one thing."

"What's that?"

"I never want to see her faint again," Jake answered.

Chapter Sixteen

Jake drove the Jeep in front of the guest house, braked, and complained, "Who's parked in my spot?"

"Looks like a new Lincoln SUV," Katherine admired.

"Katz, are you expecting anyone this morning?"

Katherine shook her head. "No, not that I know of. Just pull into the lane by the side of the house and park behind my Subaru."

Jake turned into the gravel drive, stopped, and switched the engine off. He wore an annoyed look on his face.

Katherine knew how much her husband coveted his parking space. She reassured, "It's probably somebody visiting one of our neighbors. They'll be gone soon, then you can re-park your Jeep."

Jake answered, getting out. "The street is empty. There are plenty of places to park."

A tall man with a military-style haircut climbed out of the Lincoln and stood by his SUV.

When Jake walked around the Jeep to open Katherine's door, the man approached and greeted, "Hello."

Jake asked, "May I help you?"

Katherine slid off her seat and stood next to Jake.

"My name is Sheldon Maddock. I'm a private investigator. Are you Katherine Kendall?" he asked, looking at Katherine.

"Cokenberger," Jake corrected. "Katherine is my wife. What's this all about?"

Katherine asked, "May I see your badge?"

"Actually, Ma'am, I don't carry a badge. I'm not affiliated with the police, but I do have identification." He reached into his front breast pocket and removed a leather identification holder. He extracted his driver's and PI licenses, and handed them to Katherine.

Katherine studied them, handed them back, and asked, "Why would a PI from New York be interested in us?"

"Actually, Ma'am, it's you I need to speak to."

"Okay, but not here in the driveway. Would you like to come up to my porch, and the three of us can talk there? For Indiana, it's unseasonably warm outside today. It will be nice to sit out in the fresh air," she said, not wanting to invite the stranger into her house.

"Yes, that would be fine. I'll follow you."

"We'll follow you," Jake said. He nodded toward the porch. "After you."

The PI walked up the front steps. "Where do you want me to sit?"

Katherine pointed, "How about that wicker chair in front of the window?"

The PI sat down.

Katherine and Jake sat down on the porch swing.

Katherine jumped right in. "What's this about?"

The PI replaced his IDs in his pocket. He pulled out a photograph of a woman holding a Siamese. He passed it to Katherine. "Do you recognize this cat?"

Katherine thought, *Why does this man have a picture of Abra*, then said, not answering the question, "I

don't recognize the woman, but the Siamese is gorgeous."
She handed the photo back to him.

"My client is the husband of the woman in the photograph. Her name was Olivia Lincoln."

"Was? Is she deceased?" Jake asked.

The PI nodded. "She passed away in 2010. My client is her husband, Roland Lincoln, formerly of Oyster Bay, Long Island, New York."

"Formerly?" Jake inquired.

"He lives in France now."

Katherine asked, "What does this have to do with us?"

"In 2009, Mr. Lincoln bought the Siamese, pictured in the photo, as a gift for his wife. Unknown to Roland, he bought a stolen cat from a New York City cattery. He paid a great deal of money—"

"Get to the point," Jake interrupted. "Like my wife asked, what does that have to do with us?"

Surprised by Jake's abruptness, which wasn't characteristic of him, Katherine reached over and squeezed his hand. "Let's hear him out, okay?"

Jake shifted on the swing. "Go on," he said to the PI.

"The Siamese, named Duchess, lived in Roland's household until 2013. In May of that year, Roland's wife's nurse, Julia Jackson, suffered a fatal heart attack," the PI paused, then backtracked. "After Mr. Lincoln's wife died, Roland traveled abroad. He allowed the nurse to continue living in the guest's quarters of his house, as long as she took care of his wife's beloved cat."

"That was very generous of him," Katherine commented, thinking about how she inherited her money by taking care of her great-aunt's cat. "What happened to the Siamese when the nurse died?"

"The cat disappeared. Roland never saw Duchess again."

"How did she disappear?" Katherine asked curiously.

"When the ambulance arrived to assist Ms. Jackson, one of my client's staff left the front door open. The Siamese ran out of the house."

"Aw, the poor cat," Katherine said.

"Recently, Roland learned Duchess had been found shortly after she escaped, and taken to a Long Island animal shelter."

"An animal shelter? What happened to the cat?" Katherine's brows furrowed into an uneasy expression.

"Bear with me, I'll get to that part."

Katherine assumed her best poker face. She didn't want the PI to know that she was aware that in late May of 2013, Abra was taken to a Long Island animal shelter. She wondered if Duchess, the cat in the picture, was indeed Abra. She asked, "Why wasn't the Siamese taken back to your client's house?"

"You must understand, Ms. Jackson was the cat's caretaker. When she died, no one in the household staff thought to look for the cat. Roland was overseas, so obviously he couldn't."

Jake fidgeted impatiently on the swing. Katherine squeezed his arm.

"Ms. Jackson filed a letter with her attorney to give to Roland in the event she died before he did," the PI explained. "In the letter, she wrote that Roland had unwittingly purchased a stolen cat from a Manhattan cattery by the name of Specialty Top Cats. She said the cat's real name was Abra and that she belonged to Harry DeSutter, also known as Magic Harry the Magician."

Katherine's eyes grew big with astonishment. She didn't want to tell the PI that Abra was now living with Jake and her. She saw movement in the window. Scout sat inside on the windowsill, and was drumming her paws on the glass directly behind the PI's head. Katherine mouthed the words, "Get down," and in a rare instance of Scout doing what her human asked, the Siamese jumped down.

The PI was unaware of the cat behind him, and continued, "Ms. Jackson claimed that her ex-husband, Roy Jackson, planned the theft of the cat to pay off money he owed to a loan shark."

"Who was Roy Jackson?" Katherine asked.

"For a number of years, he worked for Harry DeSutter. He was an animal trainer."

"What does Roy Jackson have to say about this?" Jake asked.

"I'm sorry to say, Mr. Jackson was murdered in 2014."

"Wow, that's terrible," Katherine said.

"I was able to track down the magician. He's retired and lives in Boston now," the PI stated, then accused, "When I contacted him, he said that in June of 2013, you, Katherine, took Abra without his permission."

"No way," Katherine said, shocked.

"That's a lie," Jake said angrily. "My wife and I went to Chicago to see Abra perform—"

"And, why was that?" the PI asked.

"Because Abra is the littermate of a Siamese my wife and I currently have."

Katherine added, "To make a long story short, in 2009, Harry DeSutter's niece, Monica, gave me Abra's

174

sister, Cadabra. In the summer of 2013, months after I'd moved from Manhattan to Erie, Monica called and said Abra had been returned to her uncle and would be performing in Magic Harry's show in Chicago. She said her uncle wanted me to see the show, and presumed I wouldn't be coming alone, so he'd leave a couple of tickets at the front desk, plus backstage passes so we could meet him and my cat's sister."

Katherine wanted to add that she'd just started dating Jake and it was their first road trip together. Jake had helped her bring Cadabra, AKA Scout, to Chicago with them. The plan was to meet Harry and ask if she could take Abra to her hotel room to see Cadabra, then later return the Siamese to Harry. She sensed the PI would think that was a ridiculous idea and only a crazy cat lady would have thought of it.

"So, let me get this straight, you went to the show in Chicago to meet Abra because you had her littermate?" the PI asked dubiously.

"Obviously you're not a cat person," Jake defended.

"Yes, exactly," Katherine said. "We wanted to see Abra perform in Harry's magic show."

"Then you used your backstage pass and stole the cat?"

"Absolutely not," Jake said indignantly. "Katz and I went backstage because Harry was furious at Abra."

"Why was he mad at the cat?"

"Because Abra didn't do what she was trained to do."

"What was she supposed to do?"

Katherine explained, "When Abra was performing on stage, she was distracted by a loud cell phone in the audience."

Jake interjected. "She leaped off the stage into the audience, and jumped from row-to-row until she found the person with the cell phone. Then she yanked the phone out of the user's hand, clutched it in her jaw, then returned to the stage, dropping it in front of Harry."

The PI smirked.

Katherine continued. "Abra's ab lib infuriated Harry, but the audience went nuts over it. One woman sitting next to us said it was the best part of the show."

"I've never heard this story before," the PI said. "What happened next?"

"Jake and I went backstage—"

"Why did you do that?" the PI cut her off. "Was the show over?"

"No, it wasn't over," Katherine answered. "When Abra dropped the phone at Harry's feet, he reached down and roughly picked her up. We didn't like the way he did that. We thought he was going to hurt her, so we used our passes to check on Abra backstage to make sure she was okay."

"Harry DeSutter told my client that you came backstage deliberately to steal the cat. I'd like to hear your side of the story."

"I can tell you exactly what happened," Katherine said. "When Jake and I went back there, a stagehand was holding an empty cat carrier. He set it on the floor. Harry was holding Abra, and from the looks of his red, contorted face, it looked like he was going to kill her."

"Why would he kill the star of his show?" the PI asked.

Katherine put her hands up. "I don't have a clue. When Harry threw Abra in the carrier, I told him I didn't like the way he did that, and he started yelling at me."

"What did he say?"

"He asked if I was the woman who had Abra's sister, Cadabra, and I said yes. He then said forcefully, 'Just take her.' Something like that. And, that's what Jake and I did. We rescued our darling Siamese from that jerk."

"Listen, folks, Harry DeSutter is not my client. Roland Lincoln is. What you've said is news to me. I'll definitely share it with Roland."

Katherine said, "Mr. Maddock, I am not in the habit of stealing cats. There was a witness backstage — Harry's manager — who can verify that Harry DeSutter told my husband and me to remove Abra from the premises. Jake and I felt that if we didn't do so, Harry was going to physically harm her, so the rest is history — we saved her."

"So, getting back to the photo I showed you. Now, do you recognize the cat?" He passed the photo back to Katherine.

Katherine glanced at the photo, then returned it to the PI. "The cat looks identical to Abra."

"My client wants justice."

"Justice, how?" she asked.

"When Roland read Julia Jackson's letter, he flew back to Oyster Bay, and went directly to the police station. He showed the police Ms. Jackson's letter, as well as written evidence that in 2009, he'd purchased a Siamese from a cattery in Manhattan. He paid thirty-thousand dollars for the cat. He showed the police a copy of the wire transfer his bank made to the cattery. He stated that the true owner of the Siamese was the magician, Harry DeSutter. I don't want to bore you with what happened next."

"No, please, continue," Katherine prodded.

"The police notified the NYPD in Manhattan. Detectives investigated the pet store and found other stolen pedigreed cats for sale."

"What happened to those cats?" Jake asked.

"They were returned to their owners."

"What about the other cats? The ones not stolen?" Katherine asked.

"They were taken to a legitimate cattery. Specialty Top Cats was shut down."

"What happened to the owner?" Jake asked.

"She went to prison for a while. She's out now, but banned from ever running a cattery again."

"Good," Katherine commented. "I bought one of my Siamese from a cattery in Manhattan, but fortunately it wasn't this pet store."

"Did Roland contact Harry and tell him he'd bought Abra?" Jake asked.

"Yes, he's spoke to the magician. It was during this call that Roland learned Duchess, also-known-as Abra, was still alive. For years, Roland didn't know the fate of his cat."

Katherine asked, "That's why you said that Roland just recently found out. He didn't know what happened to the Siamese until he read the nurse's letter?"

The PI corrected. "He didn't know all the facts until he called Harry."

Katherine said, "I'm trying to put all the pieces together. There's more to the story, right?"

"Yes, there is. Roland was thrilled that Duchess was okay. When he asked the magician if he could come and see her, Harry declined and said he didn't have the cat, someone else did."

"Is this why Roland hired you? To find me?" Katherine asked.

"Well, yes and no. Roland hired me to find out where Duchess was."

"Okay, I'm sorry I interrupted, please go on."

"Getting back to this phone conversation, Harry told Roland that he was being charged with insurance fraud because when Abra was stolen, he'd filed a claim for a large sum of money. But, four years later, when he got the Siamese back, he failed to notify the insurance company."

Jake piped in. "Oh, I get it. The nurse's letter would help the magician prove his innocence."

"Roland agreed to testify in court, if Harry would give him Duchess's new owner's name and address. Harry said he'd do better than that, he'd get the cat back."

"Unbelievable," Katherine said, disgusted. "Harry doesn't stand a chance. I'll hire the best attorney money can buy. I'll fight this."

"Let me continue," the PI said. "Harry said he'd get the cat back and sell it to Roland for thirty-thousand dollars."

Jake said, disgusted, "What a worthless jerk!"

"When my client refused, Harry reluctantly gave Roland your name and address. And, this is how I found you."

"But Harry doesn't know my address here. This is my guest house. How did you know to find me here?"

"When I checked in at the Erie Hotel and casually inquired about you, the front desk person told me."

"Small town," Jake said, not amused.

Katherine asked, "You found me. Now what? Does Roland want Abra?"

"Although as much as he loves Duchess, he said it would be difficult for him to take her to his home in France. Roland wants to be assured that Abra's owners are fit to keep her."

"Fit to keep her," Jake mocked. "Abra lives the life of Riley."

"My client doesn't know this."

"If he wants to know about us, he can Google our names on the Internet," Katherine said. "He'll find out that we're good people and not cat thieves."

"My wife has been the benefactor of dozens of charities in this town, including the new Erie Animal Rescue Center. I think that Roland would find that we are 'fit' cat parents," Jake said strongly.

"Yes, from what you've told me, it sounds like you are," the PI said, getting up. "There is one thing he asked me to do, if it's okay with you. He wants a picture of Abra in her new home."

"Give me your client's email address," Katherine said. "I'll send him one."

"Actually, he wanted me to take the pic and text it to him today."

Katherine thought fast on her feet. She didn't want the PI to know Abra was at the vet, in case he wanted to go there and try and take her. She didn't trust him. "Not possible," she answered. "I don't allow strangers in my home, especially around my cats."

"Understood," he said, reaching into his breast pocket. He removed a business card. "This is Roland's home address and his email address. Also, here's his cell phone number. He'd be so appreciative if you would send him a photo. He loved Duchess, I mean Abra, very much. Thank you for your time," the PI said, stepping off the front porch and heading to his car.

Once the PI pulled away, Katherine asked Jake, "Why were you so abrupt with that man?"

"What do you mean?" he said, getting up.

"I mean, in the beginning, I thought you were going to come unglued and throw the man off the porch."

Jake held his hand out and helped Katherine out of the swing. "Sweet Pea, I'm an old-fashioned kind of a guy. As your husband, it's my job to protect you."

"Protect me? I'm perfectly able to protect myself," Katherine countered.

"Katz, since I've known you, and I hesitate to say this, you've been a magnet for criminals."

"Unfortunately, this is true," she agreed.

"Besides, ever since we brought Abra home from Chicago, my gut instinct told me we hadn't heard the last from Harry DeSutter. Either he was going to show up and want Abra back, or he'd take us to court to get her back."

"I've always thought that, too," she sighed. "Later, I'm going to call my attorney and set up a time to talk to him about this."

185

"Good idea."

"In the meantime, I bet our kids wonder why we sat on the porch so long." She walked over to the front door, turned the key in the lock, and opened it. Five hungry felines were on the other side, and demanded to be fed ASAP.

"Back! Back!" she said, pushing her shoe through the door's opening. "Get back from the door."

Katherine walked in with Jake right behind her.

"I'll feed them," he said, walking toward the kitchen.

Lilac, Abby, Iris, Dewey and Crowie flew after him. A very sad Scout stayed behind. Katherine picked her up. "Abra is okay. We're going to go get her later. Do you want to come with us when we pick her up?"

Scout leaped from Katherine's arms, dashed to the front door, and cried a loud yowl.

Katherine's phone rang. She reached in her purse and brought out her cell. She was surprised to see the vet's name on top of the screen. She answered, "Dr. Sonny, is everything okay?"

"Everything is fine. I'm ruling out epilepsy, but I now think Abra had an anxiety attack. I've given her a mild sedative, and would like to send her home with a prescription of the same."

"A prescription?" Katherine asked.

"I've prescribed just enough pills for the rest of this week. Then, I want to see her again."

"Okay."

"I've given Abra fluids, so she's good to go."

Katherine could hear Abra shrieking in the background. "I don't think your sedative is working. She's having a royal cat fit, right?"

"That sums it up completely," he agreed.

"Thanks so much. We'll be right there," she said, hanging up.

Jake came back into the room. "Who was that?"

"Dr. Sonny. He said we can pick up Abra now."

"So much for observation. Let me guess. Abra is screaming her head off."

Katherine giggled.

"Okay, I'll get the carrier."

Katherine said to Scout, "Abra needs you to calm her down."

Scout, still positioned in front of the door, stood up on her hind legs and jiggled the door handle with her front paws. "Waugh," which sounded like 'hurry up.'"

"I take that as a yes."

Chapter Seventeen

A Week Later

Katherine sat down cross-legged on the wood floor in the living room of the guest house. She extracted items from her purse and lined them up on the floor. Seven inquisitive felines gathered around her to check out what she was doing. The collective yowls of the cats were deafening. "Inside voices, please," she said over the din.

"I give up," she said, turning the purse upside-down and dumping the rest of the contents out. Not finding what she wanted, she accused, "Okay, which one of you stole my keys?"

"Waugh," Scout cried, nuzzling Katherine with her jaw, exposing one fang.

"Magic cat, you look innocent enough. I can scratch you off the suspect list."

Abra, with her pencil-thin tail held straight up in the air, trotted over and head-butted Scout. She looked at Katherine with crossed eyes.

"Glad to see you're feeling better. You look innocent enough, too."

"Raw," Abra answered.

"But, what about you other scoundrels? Which one of you stole my keys?"

"Yowl," Iris demurred.

"Was it you, Miss Siam? What about you, Queen of the Nile?" she asked the Abyssinian.

Abby darted out of the room, and returned with a shiny object dangling from her mouth. She straddled the key ring like a spider, dropped it, then picked it up in her jaws. She headed to her favorite wingback chair to add the latest prize to her stash.

"Oh, no you don't," Katherine said, intercepting the thief. She picked Abby up, but the cat refused to let go of the keys.

"Drop it."

Abby clamped down harder.

"Now." Katherine massaged Abby's lower jaw. Finally, the Abyssinian acquiesced and dropped the keys. They fell to the floor with a loud clink.

"Chirp," Abby cried, disappointed.

Iris pounced on them and swiftly batted them under the television console.

Katherine put Abby down, and chased after Iris. "I'll fix you, my pretty." She caught the Siamese, picked her up and gave her a kiss on top of her head. Setting the cat down, she kneeled down on her hands and knees and fished underneath the console. Finding the keys, she got up.

Jake walked into the room. "What's going on in here?"

"Just another feline theft bust," Katherine laughed.

"Wish I'd had my camera."

"To take a picture of Abby?"

"No, of Scout and Abra. When I walked in, they looked like gorgeous show cats."

"Let's not mention the word 'show,'" Katherine reminded.

The mail carrier stepped on the front porch and pushed several letters through the mail slot. The cats ran to the pile. Dewey and Crowie pounced on an envelope while Iris bit it with her fangs. Scout and Abra padded over and wrestled the envelope away from the trio.

Abra grasped the letter in her jaw and brought it over to Katherine. She dropped it, then blinked an eye kiss.

"Good girl," Katherine praised.

"Must be important," Jake said. "Who's it from?"

"There's no return address."

"Open it. The suspense is killing me."

Katherine opened the envelope and removed a single, folded sheet of paper. A check fell out and twirled to the floor. Scout sprang over and stepped on it to keep the other cats from running off with it.

"What do you have there?" Jake asked Scout.

Scout pushed the check in Jake's direction. Jake picked it up. His eyes widened in shocked disbelief.

Katherine moved next to him and looked over his shoulder. "Oh, my. It's a check from Roland Lincoln."

Abra cried a raw that sounded happy.

Jake asked, "Did you see the amount?"

"Wow, thirty-thousand dollars."

"Is it a bribe?" Jake asked suspiciously.

"A bribe? What are you talking about?"

"Money to induce you to give Abra back."

Katherine scanned the letter. "Heavens no, he's donating the money to our rescue center. How kind of him. He said that we don't need to thank him, but he'd be pleased if we put a plaque on the wall with his deceased wife's name on it."

"I've forgotten her name," Jake said guiltily.

"Her name was Olivia."

"Raw," Abra agreed.

"I've got a super idea," Katherine said with a broad smile. "Lizzie and Nicholas want to add a room at their Cat Sanctuary for intakes. I'm giving them this money, so they can do that."

"You're precious," Jake said affectionately. "You can put Olivia's plaque there."

"Exactly, but I was thinking we could have Roland send us a really good picture of Olivia and Duchess. I'll have it framed, and hang it in that room."

"And, maybe a sign at the front door: Duchess welcomes you."

"I love it!"

Jake pulled out his cell phone from his back pocket. "Speaking of Roland, let's send him another picture of Abra. This time with Scout in it."

Katherine sat back down on the floor. "Scout. Abra. Come to mommy." She patted the floor. The sisters walked over with their tails intertwined. Katherine pulled them into a hug.

Jake took the picture. "Perfect," he said.

The other cats joined Katherine on the floor. Jake snapped a second picture and laughed. "Let's send that one too."

"There's something else he mentioned in the letter. He said we never have to worry about 'you know who,'" she said, talking in code, so Abra wouldn't hear Harry DeSutter's name again.

"Are you referring to the magician? Personally, I'd like to make him disappear."

Katherine laughed. "Apparently, Mr. Jerk signed some kind of legal release that he would not pursue getting Abra back. In a few days, we'll be getting a copy from Roland's attorney."

"Katz, that's a good name for him. Are you relieved that it's over?"

Katherine sighed. "I feel like a huge weight has been lifted from my shoulders."

"In that case, you'll have room for dinner," Jake joked.

"I said my shoulders, not my stomach, but I'm likin' your idea."

"Erie Hotel? Prime rib? Say about six o'clock?"

"My mouth is watering."

The cats began to yowl loudly.

Jake asked the cats, "Who wants lunch?"

The cats yowled even louder.

"Last cat to the kitchen is a rotten egg," Jake kidded. The cats thundered out of the room.

Katherine jumped up and joined them. "Looks like you're the rotten egg," she called to Jake.

Jake ran in, grabbed her in a hug. "I love you, Sweet Pea."

Katherine took Jake's face in her hands and kissed him on the nose. "I love you, too."

The End

Coming later this year . . .

The Cats that Walked the Haunted Beach

Book Ten in *The Cats that* . . . Cozy Mystery series is in the process of being written.

Katherine's best friend Colleen and Jake's cousin Daryl are finally tying the knot. Daryl wants a large wedding in Erie; Colleen prefers a small one in Manhattan. The couple can't agree on which kind it's going to be. Katz and Jake are caught in the middle. Meanwhile, Stevie's big news is out of left field and has everyone at the diner talking. Katz votes for a time-out and proposes a girls' retreat to a bed & breakfast close to the Indiana Dunes. Back in NYC, Colleen's mum is in a tizzy because she's found a vacation cabin with shoreline access to Lake Michigan. Against Katz's better judgment, she agrees with Mum's plan — only on one condition: she's bringing Scout and Abra, who become very upset when she's away from them. With the Siamese in tow, Katherine and Colleen head to the Dunes to find that Mum's weekend retreat is far from ideal. Mysterious events start happening from the beginning, culminating with a murder on the beach. It's up to Katz and her extraordinary Siamese to solve the case.

Dear Reader . . .

Thank you so much for reading my book. I hope you enjoyed reading it as much as I did writing it. If you liked *"The Cats that Stopped the Magic,"* I would be so thankful if you'd help others enjoy this book, by writing a positive review on Amazon and/or Goodreads. Please recommend it to your friends, family, and book clubs.

I love it when my readers write to me. I try to answer all emails within twenty-four hours. If you'd like to talk to me about what you'd like to see in the next book, or comment about your favorite scenes and characters, email me at: karenannegolden@gmail.com

I love to post pictures of my cats on my Facebook pages, and would enjoy learning about your pets as well.

Follow me @ https://www.facebook.com/karenannegolden

Binge reading adds zero calories. The following pages describe my other books in the series. If you love mysteries with cats, don't miss these action-packed page turners.

Thanks again.

Karen

The Cats that Surfed the Web

Book One in *The Cats that* . . . Cozy Mystery series

If you haven't read the first book, *The Cats that Surfed the Web*, you can download the Kindle or paperback version on Amazon.

With over five-hundred Amazon positive reviews, "The Cats that Surfed the Web," is an action-packed, exhilarating read. When Katherine "Katz" Kendall, a career woman with cats, discovers she's the sole heir of a huge inheritance, she can't believe her good luck. She's okay with the conditions in the will: Move from New York City to the small town of Erie, Indiana, live in her great aunt's pink Victorian mansion, and take care of an Abyssinian cat. With her three Siamese cats and best friend Colleen riding shotgun, Katz leaves Manhattan to find a former housekeeper dead in the basement. There are people in the town who are furious that they didn't get the money. But who would be greedy enough to get rid of the rightful heir to take the money and run?

Four adventurous felines help Katz solve the crimes by mysteriously "searching" the Internet for clues. If you love cats, especially cozy cat mysteries, you'll enjoy this series.

The Cats that Chased the Storm

Book Two in *The Cats that . . .* Cozy Mystery series

It's early May in Erie, Indiana, and the weather has turned most foul. We find Katherine "Katz" Kendall, heiress to the Colfax fortune, living in a pink mansion, caring for her three Siamese and Abby the Abyssinian. Severe thunderstorms frighten the cats, but Scout is better than any weather app. A different storm is brewing, however, with a discovery that connects great-uncle William Colfax to the notorious gangster John Dillinger. Why is the Erie Historical Society so eager to get William's personal papers? Is the new man in Katherine's life a fortune hunter? Will Abra mysteriously reappear, and is Abby a magnet for danger?

A fast-paced whodunit, the second book in "The Cats that" series involves four extraordinary felines that help Katz unravel the mysteries in her life.

The Cats that Told a Fortune

Book Three in *The Cats that* . . . Cozy Mystery series

      In the land of corn mazes and covered bridge festivals, a serial killer is on the loose. Autumn in Erie, Indiana means cool days of intrigue and subterfuge. Katherine "Katz" Kendall settles into her late great aunt's Victorian mansion with her five cats. A Halloween party at the mansion turns out to be more than Katz planned for. Meanwhile, she's teaching her first computer training class, and a serial killer is murdering young women. Along the way, Katz and her cats uncover important clues to the identity of the killer, and find out about Erie's local crime family . . . the hard way.

The Cats that Played the Market

Book Four in *The Cats that* . . . Cozy Mystery series

A blizzard blows into Indiana, bringing gifts, gala events, and a ghastly murder to heiress Katherine "Katz" Kendall. It's Katherine's birthday, and she gets more than she bargains for when someone evil from her past comes back to haunt her. After all hell breaks loose at the Erie Museum's opening, Katherine and her five cats unwittingly stumble upon clues that help solve a mystery. But has Scout lost her special abilities? Or will Katz find that another one of her amazing felines is a super-sleuth?

With the cats providing clues, it's up to Katherine and her friends to piece together the murderous puzzle . . . before the town goes bust!

The Cats that Watched the Woods

Book Five in *The Cats that* . . . Cozy Mystery series

What have the extraordinary cats of millionaire Katherine "Katz" Kendall surfed up now? "Idyllic vacation cabin by a pond stocked with catfish." It's July in Erie, Indiana, and steamy weather fuels the tension between Katz and her fiancé, Jake. Katz rents the cabin for a private getaway, though Siamese cats, Scout and Abra, demand to go along. How does a peaceful, serene setting go south in such a hurry? Is the terrifying man in the woods real, or is he the legendary ghost of Peace Lake? It's up to Katz and her cats to piece together the mysterious puzzle. The fifth book in the popular "The Cats that . . . Cozy Mystery" series is a suspenseful, thrilling ride that will keep you on the edge of your seat.

The Cats that Stalked a Ghost

Book Six in *The Cats that . . .* Cozy Mystery series

     While Katherine and Jake are tying the knot at her pink mansion, a teen ghost has other plans, which shake their Erie, Indiana town to its core. How does a beautiful September wedding end in mistaken identity . . . and murder? What does an abandoned insane asylum have to do with a spirit that is haunting Katz? Colleen, a paranormal investigator at night and student by day, shows Katz how to communicate with ghosts. An arsonist is torching historic properties. Will the mansion be his next target? Ex-con Stevie Sanders and the Siamese play their own stalking games, but for different reasons. It's up to Katz and her extraordinary felines to solve two mysteries: one hot, one cold. Seal-point Scout wants a new adventure fix, and litter-mate Abra fetches a major clue that puts an arsonist behind bars.

The Cats that Stole a Million

Book Seven in *The Cats that* . . . Cozy Mystery series

Millionaire Katherine, aka Katz, husband Jake and their seven cats return to the pink mansion after the explosion wreaked havoc several months earlier. Now the house has been restored, will it continue to be a murder magnet? Erie, Indiana is crime-free for the first time since heiress Katherine, aka Katz, and her cats moved into town. Everyone is at peace until domestic harmony is disrupted by an uninvited visitor from Brooklyn. Why is Katz's friend being tracked by a NYC mob? Meanwhile, ex-con Stevie Sanders wants to go clean, but ties to dear old Dad (Erie's notorious crime boss) keep pulling him back. Murder, lies, and a million-dollar theft have Katz and her seven extraordinary cats working on borrowed time to unravel a mystery.

The Cats that Broke the Spell

Book Eight in *The Cats that* . . . Cozy Mystery series

When a beautiful professor is accused of being a witch, she retreats to her cabin in the woods. Soon a man dressed like a scarecrow begins to stalk her, and vandals leave pentagrams at her front gate. The town of Erie, Indiana has never known a witch hunt, but after the first accusation, the news spreads like wildfire. "She stole another woman's husband, then murdered him," people raged in the local diner. "She uses her black cats to cast spells to do her evil deeds!" But what do the accusers really want? How is Erie's crime boss involved? In the meantime, while the pink mansion's attic is being remodeled, Katz, Jake and their seven felines move out to a rural farmhouse, which is next door to the "witch." They find themselves drawn into a deadly conflict on several fronts. It's up to Katz and her seven extraordinary cats to unravel the tangle of lies before mass hysteria wrecks the town. Murder, mayhem, and a cold case make this book a thrilling, action-packed read that will keep you guessing until the very end.

Acknowledgements

I wish to thank my husband, Jeff Dible, who edited the first draft of this book. We've been together for thirty-six years, and throughout those years, he's wholeheartedly supported my passion for writing.

Thank you, Vicki for being my editor. You are the best.

Thank you so much, Rob. Once again, you did an amazing cover.

Big hugs to Ramona, and her dog Louie, for beta reading my book.

Thanks to my loyal readers, my family, and friends.

The Cats that . . . Cozy Mystery series would never be without the input from my furry friends. My husband and I have many cats, ranging in ages from five to fourteen-years-old.

Dedication

To the sweetest Siamese ever . . . .

Iris the Second

And my brother, Bob

Made in the USA
San Bernardino, CA
03 December 2018